DEATH IN THE DARK

Skye Fargo was alone in the cabin. Not totally alone, though. He had somebody for company. A dead body. The corpse of the man who had hired him for this hellish job.

Fargo sat down, Colt in hand. He didn't have long to wait. A figure appeared in a window to his right. Fargo kept waiting. A second man appeared in the opposite window. The second man lifted a leg to climb over the windowsill, and Fargo let another few seconds go by with icy patience. He took the man still peering through the window first, and blew his head apart with a single shot. He shifted the Colt and fired again, two shots this time. Both caught the second man as he was halfway into the room. The man cried out as his body fell backward out of the window, his legs following with almost disembodied slowness.

The Trailsman heard more running footsteps outside—and he knew what he feared was true. There were more men out there, a lot more, surrounding the cabin like a noose.

Fargo was facing an army of the night—and his chances seemed zero to none of living to see the dawn. . . .

THE TRAILSMAN #153
SAGUARO SHOWDOWN

⊘ SIGNET   (0451)

BLAZING NEW TRAILS
WITH THE ACTION-PACKED
TRAILSMAN SERIES
BY JON SHARPE

☐	THE TRAILSMAN #104: COMANCHE CROSSING	(167058—$3.50)
☐	THE TRAILSMAN #113: SOUTHERN BELLES	(169635—$3.50)
☐	THE TRAILSMAN #119: RENEGADE RIFLES	(170938—$3.50)
☐	THE TRAILSMAN #121: REDWOOD REVENGE	(171306—$3.50)
☐	THE TRAILSMAN #123: DESERT DEATH	(171993—$3.50)
☐	THE TRAILSMAN #124: COLORADO QUARRY	(172132—$3.50)
☐	THE TRAILSMAN #125: BLOOD PRAIRIE	(172388—$3.50)
☐	THE TRAILSMAN #128: SNAKE RIVER BUTCHER	(173686—$3.50)
☐	THE TRAILSMAN #131: BEARTOWN BLOODSHED	(173724—$3.50)
☐	THE TRAILSMAN #133: SAGE RIVER CONSPIRACY	(173759—$3.50)
☐	THE TRAILSMAN #134: COUGAR DAWN	(175034—$3.50)
☐	THE TRAILSMAN #135: MONTANA MAYHEM	(175271—$3.50)
☐	THE TRAILSMAN #136: TEXAS TRIGGERS	(175654—$3.50)
☐	THE TRAILSMAN #137: MOON LAKE MASSACRE	(175948—$3.50)
☐	THE TRAILSMAN #138: SILVER FURY	(176154—$3.50)
☐	THE TRAILSMAN #139: BUFFALO GUNS	(176669—$3.50)
☐	THE TRAILSMAN #140: THE KILLING CORRIDOR	(177517—$3.50)
☐	THE TRAILSMAN #141: TOMAHAWK JUSTICE	(177525—$3.50)
☐	THE TRAILSMAN #142: GOLDEN BULLETS	(177533—$3.50)
☐	THE TRAILSMAN #143: DEATHBLOW TRAIL	(177541—$3.50)
☐	THE TRAILSMAN #144: ABILENE AMBUSH	(177568—$3.50)
☐	THE TRAILSMAN #145: CHEYENNE CROSSFIRE	(177576—$3.50)
☐	THE TRAILSMAN #146: NEBRASKA NIGHTMARE	(178769—$3.50)

Prices slightly higher in Canada.

THE TRAILSMAN

153

SAGUARO SHOWDOWN

by

Jon Sharpe

A SIGNET BOOK

SIGNET
Published by the Penguin Group
Penguin Books USA Inc., 375 Hudson Street,
New York, New York 10014, U.S.A.
Penguin Books Ltd, 27 Wrights Lane,
London W8 5TZ, England
Penguin Books Australia Ltd, Ringwood,
Victoria, Australia
Penguin Books Canada Ltd, 10 Alcorn Avenue,
Toronto, Ontario, Canada M4V 3B2
Penguin Books (N.Z.) Ltd, 182–190 Wairau Road,
Auckland 10, New Zealand

Penguin Books Ltd, Registered Offices:
Harmondsworth, Middlesex, England

First published by Signet, an imprint of Dutton Signet,
a division of Penguin Books USA Inc.

First Printing, September, 1994
10 9 8 7 6 5 4 3 2 1

The first chapter of this book originally appeared in *Prairie Fire*,
the one hundred fifty-second volume in this series.

 REGISTERED TRADEMARK—MARCA REGISTRADA

Printed in the United States of America

The Trailsman

Beginnings . . . they bend the tree and they mark the man. Skye Fargo was born when he was eighteen. Terror was his midwife, vengeance his first cry. Killing spawned Skye Fargo, ruthless, cold-blooded murder. Out of the acrid smoke of gunpowder still hanging in the air, he rose, cried out a promise never forgotten.

The Trailsman they began to call him all across the West: searcher, scout, hunter, the man who could see where others only looked, his skills for hire but not his soul, the man who lived each day to the fullest, yet trailed each tomorrow. Skye Fargo, the Trailsman, and the seeker who could take the wildness of a land and the wanting of a woman and make them his own.

1860, the hot, dry land the Army
still called the Department of Arizona—
where the ambitious seized the time
and the place to kill and conquer . . .

1

The big man's lake blue eyes intently watched the scene unfold below, and he used the widespread, unruly branches of the paloverde as a hiding place for himself and the magnificent Ovaro. This was the third day he watched, intrigued by what he saw. As on the other two days, the young woman rode a cinder gray quarter horse from the distant ranch to halt almost at the foot of the hill below him. She ran a hand through full, black hair worn loose, and her slender form was clothed in a white shirt and blue Levi's. She dismounted and waved a hand to a short, paunchy figure of a gray-haired man some hundred yards away. Then, with another wave, she leaped into the saddle and sent the horse into an instant gallop.

Bending low in the saddle, she raced the distance to where the man waited holding a large pocket watch on a silver chain. He consulted the watch as she skidded the horse to a halt, and held it up for her to see. They spoke for a moment, then she walked the horse back to the starting point where she repeated the dash again. She made two more, and the man timed her at each, and when she finished, they walked to where a wall of sun-dried clay stood isolated, attached to absolutely nothing. It had plainly been erected for a single purpose, and Skye Fargo watched from beneath the paloverde branches as the scene below repeated what he had witnessed the previous two days.

Four men came from the ranch buildings to join the young woman at the lone wall, which Fargo estimated to be some ten feet in height. They brought grappling hooks which they tossed to catch hold at the top of the wall and then pulled themselves up and lowered themselves down the other side. This time the young woman used the watch and had them repeat the maneuver over and over until she did the same with another four men who came from the ranch. When the second group finally finished, she took one of the grappling hooks and scaled the wall herself. Even from his distant vantage point, Fargo saw that she moved faster than any of the men. She scaled the wall five times and then took the eight men back to the ranch buildings where they engaged in what was plainly a rehearsal for an attack. Breaking into units of two or acting individually, they dashed around the corners of ranch buildings, stables, bunkhouses, toolsheds, and the main house. They flattened themselves against outer walls, sometimes crawled, and ducked around corners with guns in hand.

When they finally halted the mock attack at a command from the young woman, the day had slid into late afternoon. Fargo's eyes narrowed in thought. There was little doubt that he had been witnessing training and rehearsal for some kind of attack, and Fargo pursed his lips as the question hung in his mind. Had he run into a stroke of luck? Had he stumbled upon what he had come to find? Perhaps only a part of it, he mused. But he had to be sure. Everything was different in this dry, hot, hardscrabble land. It offered nothing in friendship—everything defensive, bristling, and harsh. He had to be sure before he moved further, and he watched the dusk begin to slide its way across the spare terrain. The weather-scoured basalt rock took on a lavender hue, and the carpet of brittlebush became blue-gray.

He realized that what happened next was his own fault, a lapse of caution. He'd let the first rule of survival slip—always be alert. His thoughts had turned to the long and twisting path that had brought him to this southwest corner of Arizona as he moved the Ovaro out of the safety of the paloverde. The four riders spotted him instantly from a little farther up the slope. They came at him at once, spreading out to cut off his flight. Fargo's hand went to the Colt at his side, but he saw the four rifles aimed at him. He could bring down two, maybe three in a shoot-out, but one was certain to blast him. Besides, he didn't want to risk a shoot-out that could mean the end of his assignment. It had become personal to him. And he wanted to learn more about the young woman and the strange series of training maneuvers.

He moved the pinto toward the four men, but kept the horse to the outside of the riders. He stayed at a walk until he drew closer to the four men when, with one motion, he dug heels into the ribs of the Ovaro and dropped his body down behind the right side of the horse. He clung with one hand on the saddle horn and put one foot in the stirrups as the Ovaro shot forward at a gallop. He heard the two rifle shots go wide over the horse and then the shouts of the men as they wheeled to give chase. Pulling himself up into the saddle again, he swerved the pinto into a narrow rock-lined passageway he had explored earlier. He raced the horse halfway up through the curving passage, pulled himself up to stand in the saddle for an instant, and leaped onto a flat ledge of rock as the

Ovaro raced on. The four pursuers appeared in moments, and Fargo, laying flat on the ledge, let the first three pass. The fourth rider, a dozen feet behind the other three, rode past the ledge and Fargo dived like a cougar on its prey.

The man fell sideways from his horse as Fargo landed on him, and hit the ground with all of Fargo's muscled weight atop him. Fargo grimaced when he heard the terrible sound of the man's neck snapping as he landed on a protruding piece of rock. Pushing to his feet, Fargo drew his Colt as he heard the sound of a horse racing back down the passageway. The third rider had found a spot wide enough to turn his horse and charge back again. The rider came into sight, then tried to rein back on his horse when he saw the figure in front of him, the Colt raised to fire. He was too late. The Colt barked, and the man clutched at his chest as he toppled from his horse. Fargo dropped to one knee, waited, ready to fire again, and listened to the sound of hoofbeats coming down the passage.

They drew closer, and his finger rested on the trigger when the hoofbeats suddenly stopped. The rider had reined to a halt just beyond sight up the curving passageway. But even on foot, there was no way he could get by without stepping into the line of fire, Fargo knew, so he waited, every muscle tensed. But the man still didn't appear. He had decided to let his quarry come to him, Fargo realized as he began to back down the passage. A dozen feet farther he turned and began to half run, half slide down the smooth rock of the passageway while his ears stayed tuned to the sound of a horse coming after him. Nearly at the bottom of the pass he heard the sound of the horse. He shot a quick glance at the walls, saw only sheer, dense rock, and began to run faster to reach the base of the passageway first and find a spot to take cover as he fired.

He had almost reached the bottom when he skidded to a halt as he saw the man waiting, the rifle to his shoulder and trained on him. Automatically, Fargo turned and started to run back up the passage when the rider came into sight, rifle raised to fire. Fargo halted, glanced back at the man at the bottom of the passage, and cursed. He was trapped. He'd be cut down by one or the other. Slowly, he lowered his Colt and waited as the men moved toward him from both sides. He'd been trapped by men who knew the terrain better than he did. The one at the bottom had come back down through another cut in the rocks and waited while the other had held his attention long enough in the passage, Fargo realized bitterly.

"Drop the gun, you sonofabitch," the man walking toward him from the bottom ordered, and Fargo let the Colt slide from his fingers. "Get back from it," the man said, and again Fargo obeyed as the man came up to retrieve the Colt and push it into his belt. Fargo took in a medium-height figure, thickset with a heavy, coarse face and lips that protruded froglike. "Call your horse," the man said, and Fargo gave the special whistle the Ovaro would know. In moments the pinto came down the passageway to halt before him. "Hit the saddle. No tricks or you're a dead man," the frog-lipped one rasped.

Fargo climbed onto the horse, and both men came up behind him. At the bottom of the hill the heavy-faced man swung onto his own horse. "Ride straight downhill," he said, and Fargo kept the Ovaro at a walk as he rode to the flat land and toward the distant ranch. As he neared it, he saw the spread was more substantial than it had appeared from a distance and certainly more opulent, the main house imposingly fashioned of stone and heavy timbers, long and flat-roofed with large windows on each side of a solid front door. The other buildings were all in good repair, he noted, freshly painted, clean, even the tool sheds in good shape. The two men brought him to the door of the main house and came to a halt. "Get down," the heavy-faced one said, and as Fargo swung from the Ovaro, he saw the young woman step from the house.

She was really quite striking, he saw at once. High cheekbones gave strength to a face that might otherwise have been simply attractive with a straight nose, doe brown eyes, a wide mouth, and full lips. Her body, slender yet full of soft gracefulness, moved with easy confidence—modest breasts nicely placed, he saw, and long legs under her Levi's. "Caught him watching us," the thick-lipped man said.

The young woman's doe brown eyes moved slowly over the big man in front of her, lingering on the chiseled strength of his face. "Spies are apparently growing handsomer these days," she commented. "Who sent you, big man?"

"Nobody sent me. I was just passing through," Fargo answered.

"Shit you were," the heavy-faced man said and thrust the rifle barrel hard into Fargo's back.

Fargo kept his eyes on the young woman. "I stopped to watch. I was curious," he said.

"A very convenient answer," she said, and he noticed she had a very direct manner of peering at him from under her black eyebrows. "What's your name?" she asked.

"Fargo . . . Skye Fargo," he said.

Her deep eyes stayed on him. "You're not from around here," she said.

"How do you know?" he tossed back.

"Something about you, something different," she said. "What are you doing here?"

"I told you, passing through. Riding by."

"To where?" she pressed.

"No place special in mind," Fargo said.

"He's lyin'," the heavy-faced man cut in.

"I suspect so, too," the young woman said, her eyes meeting Fargo's bland gaze. "Lock him up, Ed. Maybe he'll decide to talk after a few days."

"He killed Johnson and Rodrigo, trying to get away," the man called Ed put in.

"They were going to kill me," Fargo said.

The young woman frowned as she thought for a moment. "No food or water. That definitely ought to loosen his tongue in a few days," she said. She met Fargo's eyes, and her face held a kind of reluctance along with determination. "It's your choice, big man. You can talk now," she said.

"Nothing to talk about," Fargo shrugged and saw her lips tighten unhappily as she turned and went into the house. The rifle barrel prodded his back again, and he was marched forward toward a small, square structure behind the house and at the edge of a corral. While Ed kept the rifle pushed into his back, Fargo watched the other man unlock the door of the structure, and he was pushed inside. Fargo got a glimpse of a barren room that had probably once been a storage shed. A small, high window let in what little light there was left of the day. Ed slammed the door shut, and the space turned almost black as Fargo heard the padlock closing on the other side of the door. He immediately pressed one ear to the door and listened to the voices, faint yet clear enough to hear. Ed's voice came first.

"Don't go near him unless I'm here," the man ordered.

"What if he has to go. There's no place in there," the other man said.

"Fuck him," Ed growled.

"She won't like that. She'll say we should've taken him to the outhouse. You know the way she is," the other man said.

"Yeah, I know," Ed muttered. "All right, if he calls, you take him to the outhouse by the barracks, but be careful with him."

"Don't worry," the other man said. "But you know if he stays mum, she'll have us keep him until it's over. She won't go for having him killed unless she can be sure about him."

"It won't matter," Ed said. "It'll be too bad about him."

"Too bad about what?"

"About his trying to escape and our having to shoot him," Ed said and laughed. "I figure that'll happen tomorrow night." He laughed again, and Fargo listened to the sound of his footsteps hurrying away. The man had no problem with disobeying orders. He had his own plan, and he'd carry it out, that was certain. Fargo's mouth grew into a thin line. He was left with no choice now. He hadn't the luxury of waiting for another visit from the young woman, and he sank to the floor as night came to plunge the little structure into total blackness. When the moon finally rose high enough to send a pale light through the small window, he pushed to his feet and went to the door.

He called out as he pounded on it. "You out there. I've got to go. Let me out," he shouted.

After a moment of silence a voice answered. "Get

back from the door," it said, and Fargo stepped back and heard the padlock being opened. "Come on out," the guard called, and Fargo pushed the door open and stepped outside to see the guard holding his rifle aimed at him. "That way," the man said gesturing to the barracks, and Fargo saw the outhouse at the far end of the building. The guard stayed back and away from him as he walked forward, but his rifle was aimed and ready to fire. Fargo reached the outhouse and pulled the door open. "Holler afore you come out," the man ordered.

Fargo nodded, stepped into the outhouse, and closed the door after him. Instantly, he reached down and drew the thin, double-edged throwing knife from the calf-holster around his leg. He placed the blade into the palm of his hand, waited a suitable length of time, then called out. "I'm coming out." He counted on the man being a fraction less tense than when he'd opened the shed door, and that fraction was all he needed. He also knew he'd have one chance, but he had faith in his marksmanship and the accuracy of the thin blade often referred to as an Arkansas toothpick. He pushed the door half open, enough to see the guard waiting a dozen feet away. His hand came up as he pushed the door open further and, using all the strength in his arm and shoulder, he threw the knife underhand.

The blade whistled through the darkness as he stepped from the outhouse, his eyes on the guard. The man didn't see the thin blade hurtling at him until it was too late. He tried to twist aside, but the knife slammed into the side of his neck, imbedding itself to the hilt. He staggered sideways, the rifle falling from his hands. He tried to reach one hand up to pull the blade from his neck and closed his fingers around the hilt of the weapon as his strength gave out. He collapsed to the ground, his hand falling from the hilt of the blade, twitched for some thirty seconds, then lay still. Fargo ran in a crouch to the man, pulled the knife free, and wiped the blade clean on the man's shirt. He pulled the man's gun from his holster and saw it was a Remington Rider five-shot, double-action piece. It would have to do until he could get his Colt back.

Holstering the gun, he ran in a crouch to the stable where a hurricane lamp burned dimly to afford some light. He found the Ovaro in a back stall, his saddle with the rest of the gear against the rear wall, and in moments he had the horse saddled and ready to go. He led the horse from the stable and had just cleared the doors when he heard the shout and then the shot fired into the air. His eyes flickered to where he had left the guard, and he recognized Ed's thickset body bending over the figure on the ground. The alarm shot had already set lamplights on in various ranch buildings, and Fargo pulled himself onto the pinto and sent the horse into an instant gallop. He raced across the open land at the front of the ranch, stayed low in the saddle, and heard Ed shout and fire off two more shots that were far off the mark. Fargo took a low fence at full speed and raced into the night, then turned the horse up the slope of the first hill, cut to his left, and galloped up another low incline. He turned again and with the pale moon affording enough light, rode into the harsh basalt rock formations to a deep cavern he had found two days earlier.

He entered the cavern, slid from the horse, and retreated deeper into its blackness. It was unlikely they'd try to give chase in the night, and if they did, they'd never find him, he knew. With a deep sigh he loosened the horse's cinch and pulled off the saddle. They'd left the big Henry in its rifle holster on the saddle, he was happy to see, and he drank from his canteen before he spread out a blanket and stretched out. He had already made one decision. He'd be visiting the ranch again, but his way this time. It seemed more likely now than before that the handsome young woman was part of what he had come here to find. But he had to know how and why. If his guess was right, she could be the key to finding out more.

He pulled off his clothes and lay back in the near-total dark of the cavern and let his thoughts unreel backward to the strange convergence of circumstances that had brought him here, hiding in this dark cavern. He found himself reliving each event as it came alive with crystal clarity.

2

Kentucky, just south of Boone's trace along the Cumberland Gap, was a rich land heavy with old, thick cottonwoods, red cedars, butternut, and pecan. Fargo rode the Ovaro along old buffalo streets as the early Kentuckians called them, ofttimes between towering mountains and then through lush, grassy plateaus. The letter in his pocket had reached him care of General Delivery in St. Louis where he still maintained a mailing address. With the letter had come detailed instructions and the kind of money only a fool would turn down. The instructions were engraved in his mind, but he read the letter again as he rode.

The money enclosed is intended to bring you to take the job we offer but it is yours whether you decide to take the job or not. We have been told you can bring the two qualities we need, your special skills as a Trailsman and your personal integrity.

I shall explain in full when we meet. Please come as soon as you can. Time is important.

Jack Timson

The letter remained tantalizingly cryptic, and he shoved it into his pocket as he rode down an incline, heavily forested, to a grove of cottonwoods. He allowed a small smile of admiration as he spied the cottage in a tiny clearing inside the cottonwoods. The detailed instructions had been both clear and accurate. Fargo rode to a halt before the cottage and cast an eye at the dusk that had begun to slip over the land. The man who stepped from the cottage came forward quickly, a smallish yet trim figure with an even-featured face and graying hair. His gray eyes took in the pinto with a quick glance.

"Skye Fargo," he said and smiled. "We were told you ride a particularly handsome Ovaro."

"Guess you were told right," Fargo said as he dismounted.

"I'm Jack Timson," the man said and thrust out his hand. "Come inside." Fargo fell in step beside Jack Timson and found the cottage was mostly a large room with a smaller bedroom in the rear, a hearth against one wall, and a large cabinet against another. Three windows let in good light, and a sofa and two chairs occupied the center of the room. "I'm glad you're here, Fargo. I was getting worried that my letter hadn't reached you, or you decided not to respond to it," Jack Timson said.

"Outside you said *we* were told I ride an Ovaro. You used the word *we* in your letter, too. I don't see anybody but you," Fargo said.

Jack Timson's smile was broad. "The *we* refers to the government of the United States. I'm a special agent," he said, and Fargo felt his brows lift in surprise. "Of course, you're wondering why we chose this out-of-the-way spot to meet with you," Timson said.

"Bull's-eye," Fargo grunted.

"There were good reasons. We wanted to avoid your coming to Washington because Washington, deplorably, is filled with spies, loose-lipped officials, traitors, and adventurers willing to do anything for money," Timson said. As the room grew dark, he rose and lighted a kerosene lamp. "We feel certain there are people who'd try to stop us from hiring you and you from working for us."

"Shut up," Fargo hissed suddenly, and Jack Timson's eyes widened. "Horses, four, maybe six," he said as his wild-creature hearing picked up the sound.

"I didn't hear anything," Timson said.

"I did. Take my word for it," Fargo snapped, and the man's face blanched.

"My God. They found out," he whispered.

The sound of horses suddenly grew loud. "They're into a gallop." Fargo frowned and started to rise from the chair. "Jesus, hit the floor," he yelled, but Jack Timson was frozen in shocked surprise. He took a moment to react, a moment that was too long. The wild fusillade of shots burst through two of the windows, shattering glass, and as he dived to the floor, Fargo saw Jack Timson's body shudder as at least three bullets crashed into him. Cursing, Fargo rolled across the floor to one of the shattered windows and raised himself up enough to peer out and return fire. But night had descended, and he saw the galloping forms receding into the trees.

Staying low, he crawled across the floor to where Jack Timson lay in a widening pool of blood. He was still alive, and his hand closed around Fargo's arm. "Can't hold on long enough to explain," Timson said, gasping out words in pain. "Cabinet . . . left drawer . . . envelope. Deliver it. He'll explain . . ." He fell silent, but was still breathing when Fargo heard the galloping hoofbeats again. He dived forward and blew out the kerosene lamp just as another fusillade of bullets crashed through the windows. This time they shot out the third window, also. They were disappearing into the darkness again when Fargo reached one of the windows to fire back. His mouth a thin line, he moved away from the window, and the room was silent now. Jack Timson had stopped breathing. Fargo crawled to the cabinet in darkness relieved only by a strand of pale moonlight that entered the cottage. He found the left drawer of the cabinet, slowly and silently pulled it out, then saw the envelope inside. He pushed it into his pocket and crawled to a corner where he could see all three windows and the door.

He sat down, the Colt in hand. The attackers had no way of knowing if their fusillades had killed both him and Timson. They'd have to find out and there was only one way they could do that, Fargo grunted silently. He had only to wait and be ready to lower the odds a little. He sat back against the wall, his ears tuned to the silence outside. The wait wasn't long as he heard the susurrant sound of footsteps sliding along the ground, and he rose to a crouch as his eyes flicked from window to window. He cocked his head to one side, listening hard, and picked up the scrape along the sill of the second window at the right. His finger rested against the trigger when he caught the sound from the window at the opposite wall.

His lips pulled back, he waited, and the figure appeared in the window at his right, peering into the darkness of the room. But Fargo still waited and let the second man appear in the opposite window. The second man lifted a leg to climb over the windowsill, and Fargo waited again with icy patience, let another second go by, and tightened his finger on the trigger. He took the man still peering through the window first and blew his head apart with a single shot, then shifted the Colt and fired again, two shots this time. Both caught the second man as he was half into the room, still over the windowsill with one leg. The man cried out, a brief sound that stopped quickly as his body fell backward out of the window, his legs following with almost disembodied slowness.

Fargo heard sounds of running feet as the two men were pulled away, and he dashed to one of the windows and fired a shot that missed as the men reached the trees with their dead. Moving back to the corner, Fargo reloaded and allowed himself a moment of grim satisfaction. He had lowered the odds by two, but he was still trapped, and now the others knew he was very much there. They'd be watching the door and the windows, waiting for him to try to get out. Hidden in the trees at the edge of the small clearing, they'd have all the advantages of concealment and position. He had but one ally, darkness, and that would be gone if he waited till morning.

He crossed the room to the small chimney and saw it was much too narrow to afford him an escape route. Kneeling at the nearest window, he peered out, trying to see if he could spot anyone moving in the trees. But he could see nothing, and he drew back, his eyes sweeping the room again. They came to a halt on the cabinet against the one wall, and his brow furrowed as the thought formed itself. He moved to the edge of the cabinet in two long strides, put his shoulder to the flat end, and curled a hand around the edge of the base. He lifted and pushed, and it moved easily with not nearly the weight he'd expected. He slid it across the floor to the door and halted to sink down against it and wait. Timing would be important. He wanted the hanging moments just before dawn, when there'd still be enough dark to cloak him, but the day would break quickly to prevent the attackers from escaping unseen.

He stayed against the cabinet and waited as the hours slid by. They had plainly decided to wait for daybreak when they were confident they could take him if he tried to flee. It was now a waiting game, and there would be only one winner, he realized, so he stayed motionless until the moonlight faded away. He rose, then went to one of the windows and peered out to where the Ovaro was still tethered at the end of the house. His eyes roamed the sky, and he soon saw the first, distant streaks of pink tinting the night sky. The dawn would come with surprising speed, he knew. It was time for waiting to end.

Moving back to the cabinet, he squeezed his way past the tall piece of furniture and pushed the front door open. He heard the instant rustle of low branches follow, and he smiled as he put his shoulder to the cabinet and began to push it out through the door, shifting himself to walk alongside it as he maneuvered the piece outside. A volley of shots erupted at once, all slamming harmlessly into the thick wooden back of the tall cabinet. Pulling and tugging at it, he inched it along the ground toward the Ovaro as another volley of shots smashed into the back of the cabinet. A third volley broke through the weakened wood, and he felt the bullets whistle over his head and heard the sound of footsteps racing toward him. They had left the trees and were running to come up along the side and get a shot at him. But the darkness was still clinging, and he pulled away from the splintered cabinet and raced the few yards to the Ovaro.

He vaulted into the saddle, tore the tether loose,

and sent the horse streaking for the trees as he stayed low. Another barrage of bullets whistled over him. He reached the trees in seconds and reined to a halt as the dawn began to touch down over the land. The four figures, dimly lighted now, raced to the trees and their horses. Fargo's shot brought one down one as he was inches from the trees, and the man stumbled forward to land with only his lifeless legs protruding from the brush. He wheeled the Ovaro, making no attempt to be silent, and sent the horse crashing through the trees as he heard the three attackers turn to chase after him at once. He turned the horse sharply, veered to his right, and knew the three would follow. He traveled perhaps another twenty-five yards when he leaped from the saddle, landing with both feet alongside a black oak as the Ovaro charged on.

He crouched half-behind the tree trunk when the three riders came charging past in pursuit of the Ovaro. He chose the one in the lead, fired, and the figure flew sideways from his horse. The other two men instantly swung their horses away and deeper into the trees where he heard them rein to a halt. He waited, listening, and heard them start to work their way back toward him. But they were on foot now, and they had separated to come at him from two sides. He grunted, a wry sound. They were moving too quickly, their footsteps snapping dry twigs as their bodies brushed back leaves. They might as well have called out their paths, he commented silently. Amateurs—clods who knew how to pull a trigger but nothing about tracking or stalking. He chose the one moving toward him from the right, and he dropped to one knee in a clump of brush as the new day began to filter down into the woods.

His eyes swept the forest, following the sounds,

and he finally picked out the dim figure moving carefully in his direction. He tuned his hearing to the second man on the left. The man was keeping pace with his companion, both moving more or less in unison. The moment he fired, Fargo knew, one or the other would know where he crouched in the brush. He'd have time to get off only one shot at whichever one he targeted, and he cursed under his breath as he knew he'd have to let the two attackers come in closer. He concentrated again on the figure moving toward him from the right. The man had bent down as he cautiously advanced, taking a step, then pausing to listen before moving on again. The man was within range of the Colt, but still partly obscured by foliage, and Fargo remained motionless, his finger poised against the trigger of the Colt.

He swore again silently as he heard the figure on his left closing in, and with a quick glance saw the shape pushing toward him. Then suddenly, the man on his right half rose, his upper body clearly in sight for a moment. Fargo pressed against the trigger of the revolver and saw the bullet slam into the man's upper chest. The figure flew backward as a showering spray of red stained the dark green, lobed oak leaves. But the instant the shot exploded, Fargo flung himself sideways, hit the ground, and rolled as four shots hurtled into the clump of brush he'd left. He came up on one knee and saw the last man drop low behind a tree trunk.

"You're the only one left, mister," Fargo called out. "You can come out and talk to me or join the others."

After a moment of silence the voice replied. "You come out. I'll talk from here," it said.

"That wasn't the offer," Fargo said. "I don't have

to come out. I'm giving you the chance to stay alive."

"How do I know you'll keep your word?" the man asked.

"You don't," Fargo said. "But I will."

"I'm just supposed to believe that?"

"That's your call," Fargo said.

There was another moment of silence. "We both come out together, guns holstered," the man answered.

"Fair enough," Fargo said, and he slipped the Colt into its holster as he rose. He stepped forward cautiously, eyes on the figure stepping from behind the tree. The man came forward, and Fargo's glance flicked to his hands. They were empty, and he moved fully into sight to face the man and saw a thin figure, a sharp face twitching nervously. "Who hired you?" he asked.

"A man. Don't know his name. He did his dealing with Kenny, and you did in Kenny," the man said with the hint of a sneer in his voice.

"Where'd you meet this man?" Fargo asked.

"Kenny met him."

"Where'd Kenny meet him?" Fargo asked, impatience coming into his voice.

"Outside Washington," the man said.

"Kenny pay the rest of you?" Fargo questioned, and the man nodded.

"That's all I know," the man said. Fargo pondered for a moment. The man could be telling the truth. He was small-time, a hired gun. "You said if I came out to talk I could walk," the man reminded him.

"So I did," Fargo admitted.

"I talked. That's all I know," he repeated.

"Go on, mister. You bought your life," Fargo said and started to turn away when his ears caught a faint sound, metal sliding against leather. He whirled and saw the man had his gun half out of his holster. With the speed of a lightning strike, Fargo drew his Colt and fired, all before the man could bring his gun up to fire. The shot doubled the thin figure in two and, with a last rasping cry, the man toppled forward to land on the ground, still doubled in two. "Damn fool," Fargo muttered as he walked away, whistled, and waited for the Ovaro to return to him.

He pulled himself onto the horse and rode slowly through the trees until he reached the roadway that had brought him to the little cottage. He halted there and pulled the envelope from his pocket. A frown slid across his brow as he read aloud the handwriting on the face of it.

Deliver to Thomas Akins, the
White House, Washington.

The frown stayed on his brow as he returned the envelope to his pocket and sent the pinto riding northeast.

3

He had been here only once, this growing citadel, this changing, expanding capital of the United States of America and all its territories, this Washington. It had changed greatly since that visit. More streets boasted cobblestones instead of dirt. New, broad avenues had been laid down. More people strolled the streets where he admired the new brass lamps on their very tall poles. Even more fancy carriages than he remembered rolled through the streets, Stanhope phaetons, Victorias, Landaulettes, and he noted an eight-spring caleche.

The day had moved into late afternoon when he walked the Ovaro up the landscaped circle that led to the gracious house with its four stately columns. Two soldiers in full-dress blues stood at attention in front of the tall door, and a third, a sergeant, came from inside the White House as Fargo dismounted. He came to a halt and waited. Fargo showed him the envelope. "I'll take it to Mister Akins," he said.

"I deliver it, soldier," Fargo said, and the sergeant went back into the house. When he returned, a man in a black, formal frock coat and black trousers accompanied him, an austere figure with wire-rimmed spectacles on a thin, long-nosed face.

"I'm Thomas Akins," he said. Fargo handed the letter to him, and the man stared down at it for a frowning moment before returning his eyes to Fargo. "Please come with me," he said, and Fargo followed into the marbled foyer of the grand house where Thomas Akins led the way into an oak-paneled study and closed the door. He opened the envelope, then took out a sheet of paper and held it up. It was blank on both sides, and Fargo saw Thomas Akins tighten his lips. The man turned his eyes on Fargo. "How did Jack Timson die?" he asked, and Fargo realized the blank sheet inside the envelope had delivered its own coded message.

"Gunned down a few minutes after I got to his place," Fargo said. "Somebody was waiting, watching his place, knew he was expecting me. They hit fast and hard. He went down with the first volley."

"Poor Jack. He was a good man, damn their souls," Thomas Akins said.

"Hired guns. I took care of all of them," Fargo said. "Timson's last words were that you'd be explaining what this is all about. I'd sure as hell appreciate that."

"Yes, I imagine you would," Akins said. "But I'm going to leave that to someone else. Please wait here." He hurried from the room only to return in moments. "This way," he said, and Fargo followed him down a short corridor into a large, stately room with maroon drapes and Irish lace curtains on the tall windows. A man rose from behind a long, claw-footed, Duncan Phyfe desk. He stood six feet tall with bright, blue eyes and an unruly tuft of hair rising from the front of his shock of white hair, not unlike a small jet of white flame. He wore a stock around his neck with a flaring white tie to match and carried his head with a slight tilt to one side. "Mr. James Buchanan, President of these United States," Thomas Akins announced and the

President took a quick step forward and thrust out a hand.

"My pleasure, Fargo," he said.

"My honor, Mr. President," Fargo returned.

"I'm sorry about all the trouble you've already had without knowing anything about this. You must feel as though you're lost in the wilderness," Mr. Buchanan said.

"I'm seldom lost in the wilderness, sir," Fargo said. "But I sure am here."

President Buchanan's blue eyes held an instant twinkle. "Of course you're not. That's why we sent for you. You're here because of a situation that ought to be simple enough, but is turning out to be far from simple in any way. Please sit down, Fargo." Fargo sank into a straight-backed chair with a seat covered in maroon material and glanced quickly around the big room as the President returned to his chair behind the desk. It was finely furnished, and he'd heard that Buchanan had tossed out all the French-made furniture and replaced it with the work of American craftsmen. "You by any chance ever hear of a man named Rolando Vargas, Fargo?" Buchanan asked.

"No, sir," Fargo said.

"Didn't think it likely you would have," the President said as he sat back in the chair. "He's of Mexican birth, but he operates somewhere in the southwest corner of the Arizona Territory. He's training and outfitting an army to invade Mexico and overthrow the present Mexican government."

"Sounds like a pretty big order," Fargo commented.

"Not as big as you might think. All he has to do is establish a good foothold for himself. Lots of people inside Mexico will flock to him because they hate the present government headed by Benito

Juarez, a very touchy little man. Relations with Mexico and the Juarez government have been, at best, strained. Do you know what would happen if an army, trained and equipped on American soil, were to invade Mexico?"

"I guess it could make all kinds of hell break loose," Fargo murmured.

"You can say that again," Buchanan agreed. "Benito Juarez might well consider it a hostile act. He could be pressed into actual hostilities by forces inside his own government. His hand could be forced."

"And you don't want that," Fargo said.

"Not at any time and especially not now," the President said. "I'm sure you've heard that there is considerably more than talk of a secession by the southern states. If that happens, it'll be Mr. Lincoln's problem, but until he's inaugurated, it's also mine. In fact, I've discussed everything we're talking about here now with him."

Fargo turned to Thomas Akins as the man entered the conversation. "There are forces that would welcome a new Mexican–American conflict. They would like to see us embroiled in hostilities with Mexico. Such an occurrence would make us commit sizable forces that might be needed elsewhere," Akins said. "These forces don't want Rolando Vargas stopped. They want him to be left alone to provoke a new Mexican–American conflict."

"You're saying they knew Jack Timson had sent for me and had their hired guns waiting to take us both out," Fargo ventured.

"It's a very educated guess," Akins said. "There are no secrets in Washington, or at least damn few. I'd say what happened in Kentucky proves that."

"It might, unless they were hired by this Rolando

Vargas. He'd want to end any attempt at stopping him," Fargo suggested.

"Highly unlikely. We don't believe he has any inside connections in Washington. He seems to be operating wholly in southwest Arizona," Akins said.

"But he's getting his financing from somewhere," the President cut in. "That's one of the things we want you to find out. Where is he getting the money to build his little army? If we knew that, we might be able to cut off his source."

"What are the other things?" Fargo queried.

"Is Vargas ready to strike? What kind of a force has he put together? Where are they?" Akins said.

"Where are they?" Fargo frowned. "Hell, that ought to be easy enough. You can't hide an army, even a small one."

"That would seem so, but we sent two agents, individually, to find that out. Before they disappeared, they sent back reports that they hadn't been able to find his force," Akins said.

"Of course, they didn't have your skills, Fargo," the President put in. "Still, it seemed to us they ought to have been able to find something. Maybe they did, finally, and never lived long enough to report back to us."

"And last, we want you to find out if Vargas can be stopped. We have a troop stationed at Gila Bend, but it is a small force, no more than a few hundred men. Would they be enough, we have to know," Akins said. He finished the sentence when a servant entered the room and lighted the lamps, and Fargo realized he hadn't noticed how dark the room had become as night descended. "There are some other details, things we'll furnish you in the morning if you agree to take the assignment," Akins said. "You've already found out it will be very dangerous."

"Take the night to decide," Buchanan said. "We've a carriage waiting to take you to a private residence here in Washington where you'll have a fine meal and a fine night's rest. You can give us your answer in the morning. Of course, we hope you'll accept."

"We're taking these extraordinary precautions because we don't want you settling in anywhere in Washington. As we said, and as you've already found out, there are few secrets here. By now, the people who tried to kill you and Jack Timson in Kentucky know they only half succeeded," Thomas Akins said.

"We'll put your fine Ovaro up in the White House stables."

"Sounds as if we'll both be well treated," Fargo said.

"Our carriage is waiting to bring you back in the morning. If you take the assignment, we'll finish the details then," Akins said.

"Thank you for carrying through till now. Many men would have turned away after what happened in Kentucky. We appreciate that," President Buchanan said, and after a final handshake Fargo walked from the room with Akins. The President's aide watched him leave from the door, and Fargo paused at the Ovaro to take his personal pouch before stepping to the waiting carriage, a black, closed, two-passenger coupe with the driver sitting high up front. Fargo entered the carriage, and the driver rolled away immediately. Settling back, Fargo watched the tall, brass street lamps create little oases of light in between the dark stretches.

When the carriage rolled to a halt, he stepped out in front of a town house, brick with a polished wood door that opened as he approached. A young woman held the door open for him, tall and statuesque, clothed in a floor-length hostess gown of smooth, white material. She was attractive, with a small nose, dark brown hair, full lips, and a well-tanned face with light brown eyes. "Welcome, Fargo. I'm Carole Wyman," she said with a warm smile.

She closed the door behind him as he stepped into a foyer with dim lighting, but not so dim he couldn't see the low, folded-over neckline of the dress that let him glimpse the long line of her breasts. She led him through a white and gold dining room with a beautiful crystal chandelier that lighted a table set for two and into a large, wood-paneled bedroom. "You can leave your things here and join me in the dining room," the young woman said. "I suspect you must be hungry."

"Come to think of it, I am," Fargo said, set his pouch down, and watched Carole Wyman walk from the room, a beautifully slinky walk, hips hardly moving. Fargo opened the pouch, put on a fresh shirt, and washed up in a small, adjoining bathroom. When he returned to the high-ceilinged dining room, Carole sat at the table to the left of the place set for him. She poured wine from a carafe as he sat down, and when he tasted the liquid, he found it to be as rich and warm in flavor as it was deep and red in color. A servant, an elderly black man, entered with a silver tray and served chopped pieces of venison cooked in a cream sauce. "I sure didn't expect this kind of treatment," Fargo observed as Carole refilled his wine glass.

"You're very important, I'm told," Carole said. "My job is to see that you have a pleasant, relaxing evening."

"You're doing just fine, honey," Fargo said between bites.

"I imagine you've received all the information

they can give you about Rolando Vargas," the young woman said.

"Not yet, but then I haven't signed on yet," Fargo said. "I see you know about this Vargas hombre. How come?"

"Just little things I happened to hear," she said.

"Akins use you a lot for special entertaining?" Fargo questioned.

"Not a lot," she said.

"What other little things did you happen to hear about Rolando Vargas?" Fargo questioned, wondering silently if Carole Wyman might tell things he hadn't been told.

"Only that he's up to something they want stopped and they contacted you for help," Carole said, her smile suddenly mischievous. "I've heard a few things about you, too," she remarked.

"Such as?"

"That you're the very best on the trail," she slid at him. "And maybe the very best in bed."

"Where'd you hear that?" he asked, finishing his wine.

"A man like you gets his own reputation. A girl like me hears things all over," she said. "Though I never expected I'd be meeting you."

"You shouldn't believe everything you hear," he told her.

"I don't," she said and tinkled a small bell on the table. The servant came in and began clearing away the dishes. "I'm sure you're tired," Carole said as she rose.

"I can use some sleep," he said.

"I hope everything was fine," she said. The question didn't fit the self-assurance of her beautifully gowned, contained figure.

"It was," Fargo said.

"Tell Akins and the President if you have an opportunity," she said, and he nodded. "A good word never hurts." She flashed another quick, warm smile and helped carry the last of the dishes away.

"Thanks and good night," he called to her. "It was real delicious."

"My pleasure," she returned from the kitchen. He rose and found his way back to the bedroom. The big double bed beckoned invitingly, and he undressed and slipped naked under the top sheet as he pondered the strange succession of events that had brought him here. It had been a day to remember, to say the least. One didn't meet a president of the United States every day. Most people would call it an honor to be personally asked by the President to take on an assignment. It was indeed an honor, he conceded. But sometimes being honored was almost a sure ticket to being dead. He'd seen that often enough, and so far this affair had all those earmarks about it. Yet he'd put his neck on the line for far less money, he reminded himself. And getting the chance to be a part of history had its appeal, he admitted. He was still turning thoughts in his mind when he heard the faint knock on the door.

"It's open," he called, sitting up and frowning as the tall figure in the white gown entered the room. Carole Wyman came straight to the edge of the bed, and he saw her eyes travel across the muscled symmetry of his torso. With a slow motion of one hand she undid a clasp, and the white gown opened. A wriggle of her shoulders and it fell away as Fargo stared at a curvaceous figure, completely tanned, with modest breasts, nicely turned full cups and very dark red nipples on a slightly lighter red areolas. Short-waisted with a prominent rib cage and rounded hips, a small, convex belly curved into a neat triangular patch that grew down to the bottom of the V where legs that seemed longer than they were because of their thinness took over.

"Don't look so surprised, Fargo," Carole Wyman said.

"It's been a day of surprises. Guess I shouldn't be taken by one more," Fargo said. "This part of your orders to convince me to take on the job?"

"They didn't give me any orders, just no restrictions," she said as she slid into the big bed with him. He felt himself responding at once to her tanned, warm body as she turned to him, and his hand curled around one full-cupped breast. Her skin was soft, her breast slightly spongy to the touch, but the prominent dark red nipple very firm. He felt her hand reach down and close around his already throbbing erectness. "Oh, yes. Oh, jeeeez," she murmured, and he felt a tremor go through her. Her hand remained closed around him as she turned onto her back and his mouth found one soft breast. He pulled gently on it, lips closed around the dark red tip, and Carole Wyman gave out tiny gasps though her fingers stayed closed around him. Her hips made small lifting motions, the senses anticipating, and he continued to caress her breasts with his tongue. "Yes, yes, oh, please, yes," Carole said, and suddenly her voice took on a new softness and she was still holding him, pulling at him now as her legs fell open.

"Take me, oh, please, now, now," she murmured, and she pulled him toward her as her pubic mound thrust upward again, little motions of frantic wanting. He slid forward, and her thin thighs came around him, but he was surprised to feel the dryness on them when he'd expected at least dampness. But Carole Wyman's dark portal thrust upward to meet him, wide and warm and her hips thrust upward, wanting all of him, and she was screaming now with each heaving motion. Her hands pulled his face forward against her breasts, and there was no slow pleasures of the flesh for Carole Wyman, no gathering of passion. She was all instant explosion, the flesh demanding immediate gratification, and he realized he was surprised at her intensity even as he was carried along by her headlong wanting.

Her screams had become almost constant, one following the other as her legs held tight around him, and he answered her demands with harsher and harsher thrusts. "Yes, yes, yes, oh, yes, more, oh, more," she cried out, and he felt himself unable to hold back, unable to do anything but match her frantic pumping. He exploded with her, and she screamed and screamed again, her voice filling the room. He felt her contractions around him grow weak, finally subsiding as did his own pulsating erectness. But Carole continued to cling to him and scream, taking short gasps for breath between screams, holding her tanned body tight against him. He frowned down at her, surprised again. She went on as if it hadn't ended, ecstasy hadn't ceased, arms and legs clinging desperately to him, her screams continuing. She took a breath between screams, and his acute hearing caught the split second of sound, the door being opened.

His reactions were unplanned. There was no time for planning, thinking, deciding. There was only time for instinct, the snap of automatic reactions. He rolled with Carole attached to him as a limpet clings to a rock, off the edge of the bed to his right. His gun belt lay on the floor at the right of the bed, where he always put it. He landed alongside it, Carole Wyman shaking loose as they hit the floor, and he heard three shots slam into the bed. But the Colt was in his hand, and he saw the two men in the doorway. He fired from almost a prone position, and the man on the right went down first. The second one swung his gun, tried to draw a bead on the figure on the floor, but Fargo fired again and the man fell forward atop the other intruder.

Fargo turned to Carole Wyman who had slid back from him, and he was just in time to see her fling the small chair at him in a sideways motion. He got an arm up, took the force of the chair on it, but still fell backward. He glimpsed her naked form streaking past him, then shot one arm out and closed his hand around her ankle. She fell sprawling face forward, and he pushed to his feet, grabbed a handful of her hair, and yanked her back. "Now who the hell are you, dammit?" he hissed.

"None of your damn business," she said, and her breasts bounced as she swung at him, trying to claw at his eyes. He pulled back, sank a short blow into her stomach, and she collapsed in two with a gasp of pain. She was holding her stomach with both hands, on her knees on the floor, as he pulled on clothes. When he had his gun belt strapped on, she regained her breath enough to straighten up, and he yanked her to her feet.

"Get dressed," he said, and she picked up the white gown and slipped it around her, fastening the clasp at the waist as she glowered at him. "Any more company expected?" he asked.

"No," she said, and the Colt pressed into her back, he walked her through the dining room to the front door. He paused, peered through the small side window, and saw that the black closed coupe was still waiting outside, the driver in his high seat. "Move . . . walk outside," Fargo said as he opened the door. She stepped out, and he hung back a moment, the Colt raised. The driver turned his head and saw Carole Wyman come from the house and pause. He beckoned to her.

"*Go!*" she screamed, and Fargo saw the man's eyes widen for an instant. He turned to the horses, started to snap the reins when Fargo stepped out behind her.

"Do that and you're a dead man," Fargo called. The driver stopped, the reins in midair, and then let his hands fall back into his lap. Fargo started to walk forward with the young woman in front of him when he saw the driver yank a pistol from under his cape. The Colt barked instantly, and the man toppled headfirst and sideways from his high seat to land lifelessly on the ground beside the front wheel of the coach. Fargo pushed Carole. "Get up," he said.

"I'd rather ride inside," she said.

"I'm sure you would," he grunted and prodded her with the barrel of the Colt. She climbed up onto the small seat, and he followed her up, holstered the gun, and sent the horse moving forward. He turned the carriage and headed back to the White House through the dark streets. Glancing at Carole, he saw she sat stiffly, hands folded on her lap, eyes staring straight ahead, looking regally incongruous in the coachman's seat. "You know, for a while there, I would have sworn you were enjoying it," he said.

"Would it make any difference if I said I was?" she asked, glancing at him.

"No," he said. "You're too good an actress to believe twice." She fell silent and returned to staring straight ahead, not moving when he drove up before the White House. The two soldiers by the door raised their carbines. "Wake up Thomas Akins," Fargo said.

"At this hour, mister? No way. He'd have our heads," the one said.

"He'll have them if you don't wake him. Tell him Skye Fargo's here," Fargo said. The two soldiers exchanged uncertain glances, but one left and went inside the stately house. He took a while to return, but when he did, Thomas Akins was with him, wearing only trousers, slippers, and an undershirt. The man's eyes went to Carole in her white hostess gown.

"Come inside," he said, and Fargo swung down from the coach and pushed Carole into the foyer ahead of him. Akins had one of the soldiers come inside also and turned to face Fargo.

"Meet Carole Wyman," Fargo said.

"Wyman?" Akins half smiled. "We know the young lady as Carole Jenkins and Carole Smith." He fastened his eyes on the young woman. "When did you become Carole Wyman, my dear?" he asked.

"Recently," Carole said, absolutely unflustered, perhaps even a trifle bored.

"Whoever she is, she set me up to be killed," Fargo said.

"Ridiculous. They were two burglars who burst in just when you happened to be screwing me," she said. "You can't prove anything else."

"Hell, the whole thing was a setup, from the carriage that brought me there to your little masquerade," Fargo said.

"It was our carriage," Akins interrupted. "They put their man in place of our driver, whom I'm sure we'll find murdered someplace."

"You can't make any of this stick," Carole said. "I'll say he came to see me on his own. It'll be my word against his. Nobody's alive to say different."

"Carole is an agent for Colonel Drysdale of the

Virginia Militia. As I said, we've met up with her before," Akins said and motioned to the soldier standing by. "Take her into custody," he said. Another voice cut in.

"Perhaps we'll hold onto her longer this time," it said, and Fargo turned to see President Buchanan in a maroon bathrobe, the tuft of hair on his head standing higher than usual. Carole walked from the house with the soldier, showing not the least bit of concern, Fargo noted. Buchanan beckoned for Fargo and Akins to follow him into the main room. "We're terribly sorry this happened," he said, turning to Fargo. "We hope it hasn't decided you against helping us. We'll raise the pay."

"I've nothing against that," Fargo said. "I'll take the job. I've been damn near killed twice, and that gets my dander up. But I don't want to wait around this town. I want to ride out tonight, before anybody decides for another try."

"I'll have your horse brought around," Akins said and hurried from the room. The President sat down behind his desk and took out a piece of paper and a long quill pen.

"The commander of our troops at Gila Bend is Major Harvey Grady. But as I told you, he doesn't command more than two hundred men," Buchanan said as he wrote, and Fargo made a mental note of the major's name.

"Isn't it likely that Vargas is getting his financing from the same sources that want him to provoke a new Mexican–American conflict, the same nice folks who tried to kill me tonight?" Fargo suggested.

The President paused in his writing and returned a wry smile. "A logical assumption, Fargo, that proves that logic is not always logical," he said, and Fargo frowned back. "We know the secessionist forces want to see him provoke the Juarez government, but they don't have the money to back him. They're desperately trying to raise money for the troops, arms, and supplies they'll need if secession occurs. They've been trying to get the British to advance them loans on cotton shipments. They want to take advantage of whatever trouble he might stir up, but they're in no position to back him. We're convinced he's getting his financing from some other source."

"Things aren't always what they seem to be," Fargo said, the President's explanation an example of that old truth. He sat back and watched as Buchanan finished his letter, reached into his desk and took out a round, heavy iron mold, and pressed it down hard onto the piece of paper. He handed the note to Fargo when he finished.

"Signed with my signature and imprinted with the presidential seal," he said, and Fargo read the note:

To Whom It May Concern:

This will introduce Mr. Skye Fargo who has undertaken a special mission for me. Please give him every courtesy and cooperation.

James Buchanan
President of These United
States of America

"Use it whenever and wherever you want, Fargo," Buchanan said. "I'm also sending a courier to Major Grady at Gila Bend, telling him he may be hearing from you."

"Very good," Fargo said and rose to his feet.

"Good luck," Buchanan said.

"Thank you, sir. I make my own luck," Fargo said and drew an appreciative chuckle from James Buchanan as he left. Thomas Akins waited at the front door.

"Your horse is waiting," the man said. "We'll send your check to the General Delivery office."

"That'll be fine," Fargo said and left after a quick handshake. As he strode outside where the Ovaro waited, he saw Carole Wyman about to be placed inside an army prisoner van, four soldiers alongside her. He paused as he passed her on his way to the Ovaro, and she smiled at him, a private amusement in the smile.

"I did enjoy it," she said.

"I almost did," he said.

"Go to hell," she snapped and stepped into the closed van.

4

The crystal-clear pictures came to an abrupt end in his mind, and Fargo was back in the near-total darkness of the cavern. It had been a long ride from Washington, but there had been no further incidents. He found this land to be as it always had been, bristly, hot, and dry, the land the Indians had aptly named *Arizona*, their name for "Place of the Little Springs." Even before reaching this southwest corner that abutted Mexico, he had had enough of bur sage and brittlebush, yucca, and hedgehog cactus, as well as the creote bushes, unruly paloverde, ajo oak, and juniper.

Yet there was beauty in this land, its own special kind of beauty, the light pink of the Fairy Duster, the burnished gold of the Mexican poppy, the scarlet of the Trumpet Bush, and the coral of the Globe Mallow. Even the giant saguaro held its own aloof, timeless kind of beauty. It was a land that made him understand the crafty hardiness and the cruelty of the Chiricahua Apache. He was grateful his trip hadn't brought him into contact with the Chiricahua, not this far, at least. He wanted to concentrate on his search, and now the young woman and the strange maneuverings on her land. He closed his eyes, pushed away thoughts, and let tiredness sweep over him in the safety of the cavern.

He slept into the day, and it was past noon when he woke. Not that he knew that in the darkness of the cave where only a glimmer of day filtered in. But when he walked outside, he saw the sun moving past the noon sky. They had probably stopped trying to find him by the morning's end, and he found a trickle of water coming down a side of rock, washed in it, and filled his hat to let the Ovaro drink. He rode carefully through the formations of basalt rock and red clay, staying away from the ranch on the plateau until evening came to darken the land. When it seemed dark enough to be safe, he moved from the hills and slowly approached the flat land where the lights still burned in the ranch buildings. He slid from the saddle alongside a cluster of jojoba and settled down next to the little dark green leaves. He waited, let all the lights go out in the compound below, then waited further.

He wanted the ranch to be wrapped in sleep before he went down to take the young woman out. It was more likely than ever that she was part of Vargas's people, but he wanted to be certain, though he couldn't think of any other reason for the training maneuvers he'd watched for three days. He'd let another two hours pass when he began to nose the Ovaro down to the dark, still buildings. He was nearing the ranch, trying to make the best of the scant cover afforded by a line of mesquite when he swore softly and yanked the horse to a halt. The barn door had opened, and a man emerged, leading a horse.

Fargo recognized the broad, thickset figure of Ed and watched as the man continued to lead the horse until he was a good fifty yards from the buildings. He climbed onto the horse then and set out in a fast canter heading south. Fargo's lips tightened for a moment as he made a quick decision. He swung the pinto around and followed Ed. The unexpected development held too much promise to let pass, and he hung back, far enough to be out of sight, and let the sound of the man's horse be his guide. Ed continued to head due south toward the Mexican border, and almost two hours had passed when Fargo found himself following the trail through a dry, gravely wash that sloped upward on both sides. In the moonlight the giant saguaro seemed like so many sentinels with their arms upraised.

The wash began to rise, and Fargo slowed as he heard the sound of Ed's horse go to a walk and finally halt. Fargo spied a cut in the side of the rock slope and dismounted, led the Ovaro into the cut, and left the horse loosely tethered to a small sprig of rock shrub. He went back down to the bottom of the wash and climbed upward on foot to where the wash leveled off to become a basalt plateau dotted with creosote bush and small growths of ajo oak. Ed had halted, staying in the saddle, plainly waiting, and after only minutes Fargo heard the sound of approaching horses. He crept in a crouch to reach the cover of one of the oaks not more than twenty-five feet from where the man waited.

The sound of the approaching horses took shape and became two riders who drew up alongside Ed. "Tomorrow night," Ed told them. "I don't know who that bastard was that got away, but I don't want to take any chances. Tomorrow night."

One of the men handed Ed a small sack tied at the top. "As agreed, half now, half on delivery," he said. Ed took it and pushed it into his jacket pocket.

"Same time, right here," he said, turned his horse, and rode away. Fargo waited, let the other two men ride back the way they had come and then hurried back to retrieve the Ovaro. He rode after Ed and closed in on the man, but stayed back as the man held a steady pace, retracing his steps. When he reached the ranch, the dawn hovered over the tops of the Growler Mountains just to the north. It'd be suicide to try to get to the young woman now, Fargo realized, so he turned away and rode to the hideaway cavern as the dawn broke. He unsaddled the horse, pulled off his clothes, and lay down on his bedroll in the cool dark of the cave.

He admitted to being more than a little curious about the man's secret meeting. There was to be another, and Fargo toyed with the thought of following him to it. Perhaps he'd learn more, he mused, and pushed the thought aside, but with difficulty. Getting hold of the young woman was still the first objective. She plainly ran the operation, whatever it was, and Fargo decided he'd wait and watch Ed leave and then go after her, with one less of her crew to give him trouble. Decisions made, he closed his eyes and let sleep come to what had been a sleepless night.

Once again, he slept deep into the morning, and when he woke and went outside, he found the little rivulet of water was still coursing down the rocks, but with only half the strength. He washed quickly, taking advantage of its grudging benefaction while it still lasted, filled his canteen, and let the horse drink before riding slowly on through the tiered rock formations. He saw the small forms of darkling beetles and scorpions scurry out of his way as he stayed clear of the ranch area though he was certain the training maneuvers he had witnessed were going on again. Finding a rock ledge, he surveyed the terrain, noting the numerous small washes and passages that led into and from each.

This land was hard and harsh, made of rust-colored stone and gray volcanic rock, and yet there were clusters of pale yellow acacia flowers and silvery wild zinnias, reddish, big queen butterflies, and delicate blue butterflies and, scattered amongst cindery soil, the pale pink blossoms of hedgehog cactus.

Circling higher, he glimpsed a half-dozen bighorn sheep and dozens of antelope jackrabbits. A roasted rabbit dinner appealed at him at once, but he didn't dare bring down one of the creatures, aware that a shot would echo through the rock-rimmed draws for God knows how far. He circled back and discovered another way to return to the cavern from behind, a crevice barely wide enough for the Ovaro to squeeze through. When he again began to make his way downward toward the ranch, the lavender dusk had settled and night was blanketing the land before he halted within sight of the ranch buildings. He drew close again, then dismounted to wait once more.

The time had come for the man to leave, and Fargo saw the door of the main house open this time and two figures emerge. He stared, a frown digging deep into his brow. One of the figures was the young woman, but she was gagged, a cloth over her mouth and hands tied behind her back. The thick figure of Ed followed, holding onto her as he pushed her forward. Fargo's eyes went to the stable as it opened and a rider came out leading a second horse. He stopped beside Ed who swung onto the horse and pulled the young woman onto the saddle in front of him. With the second man riding alongside, he sent the horse northward as he had the night before. Fargo stared after the horses, the frown still deep on his forehead—one more surprising twist in what had become a series of surprising twists. This one was perhaps the most unexpected of all, he murmured to himself as he climbed onto the Ovaro and followed the two horses through the night.

It was a long ride before Fargo saw the wash come into sight and then the long plateau beyond it. He dismounted, paused a moment beside the Ovaro inside the narrow cut, and his hand rested on the butt of the Remington Rider at his hip. He grimaced unhappily. He wasn't familiar enough with the gun, and he didn't think much of the Remington's accuracy in the first place. He pulled the big Henry from its saddle holster and, holding the rifle loosely in one hand, left the cut and moved up the end of the wash to the plateau, dropping to one knee behind the cluster of ajo oaks. The two men stood on the ground beside the young woman, and Fargo saw Ed yank the piece of cloth from around her mouth. She stared at him, more hurt disbelief than anger in her face.

"Why, Ed? I don't understand. Talk to me," she said.

"Shut up," the man snapped. "You wouldn't understand." The young woman stared at him, her long, black hair moving in a light breeze, and Fargo had a chance to see that she wore the top of a nightgown tucked into her Levi's. The sound of horses approaching turned her eyes from Ed, and Fargo watched two riders appear. They drew to a halt and stared down at the young woman. "Delivery in full," the thickset man said.

One of the man tossed him a small sack, a duplicate of the one he'd turned over the previous night. "Payment in full," he said.

"Is that what this is all about, Ed?" the young woman asked, hurt in her voice. "Money? Selling your soul for thirty pieces of silver?"

"Goddamn right," Ed said. "Only I'm not selling my soul. I'm getting something instead of a gut full of lead from going along with your crazy ideas."

"You're a traitor and a coward," the young woman said, her voice rising.

"That's enough of this shit," one of the two men on horseback interrupted and gestured to Ed. "Kill her," he ordered.

"That wasn't part of the deal. I delivered her. You can kill her. I thought she'd be worth something to you alive," Ed said.

"No. Our orders are to kill her," one of the men answered.

"Where?" Ed questioned.

"This is as good a place as any," the man replied, and Ed shrugged as he turned away. The man started to draw his pistol, and Fargo's eyes went to the girl for an instant. She remained perfectly still, head high in defiance.

"*Roñoso!*" she flung at him in Spanish. Fargo raised the big Henry to his shoulder and took aim. The one with the pistol out had to be first, and he fired. The man flew backward over his horse's rump as a spray of red erupted from his chest. The others whirled in astonishment, but Fargo fired again, and the second man on horseback flew from his saddle, sideways. The man with Ed had his gun out and fired wildly in the direction of the ajo oaks, and Fargo took a moment to see the girl start to run and fall as Ed tackled her. He swung the rifle a fraction to the right, and the third man screamed as the heavy rifle slug tore into his belly, and his second volley of shots went harmlessly into the cindery ground. Fargo brought the rifle back to where Ed lay on the ground, holding the young woman in front of him, half over his body. He had his six-gun out and pressed against her cheekbone.

"Come out with your hands empty or she gets it," the man called.

"She gets it, you get it," Fargo said. "Count on it."

The man thought for a moment and pushed himself to his feet, holding the young woman in front of him. "I ride out of here with her. Give me five minutes, and I let her go," he offered.

Fargo said nothing and let the man think he was considering the offer. In reality he was only considering when he'd shoot. The man wouldn't let her go in five minutes. He couldn't afford to do that. Fargo's eyes narrowed as he let thoughts find their own decision. "All right. You've got a five-minute head start," Fargo said, and Ed backed toward his horse, holding the young woman in front of him. Fargo saw her staring at him, as much wonder as there was fear in her eyes. Fargo stayed unmoving, the rifle raised, one finger on the trigger, and he watched as Ed reached his horse, paused, and Fargo grunted inwardly. Ed hadn't figured out how he'd keep the girl as a shield and get himself and her onto the horse. Fargo's finger stayed resting against the trigger of the rifle as he saw the man move the pistol from the girl's cheek and place it against the top of her head, pushing the barrel through the thick black hair. The pistol, Fargo saw, was his Colt.

Keeping the gun barrel against her head, Ed used his other hand to pull himself onto the horse. He was a clear target, but Fargo had to force his finger not to tighten on the trigger. The gun was still at the young woman's head. The shot that could easily blast Ed away could also make his finger pull the pistol trigger as an automatic, physical reaction. Fargo's lips drew back as he forced himself to wait. "Turn around," he heard Ed order the girl, holding the gun at her head as she did, then reaching down with his other hand for her. "Get up here," he said. She reached up, started to obey, and for an instant, the man's gun moved from her head. She flung herself backward in a twisting motion, and she was still in midair when Ed fired, his shot missing her by a fraction of an inch.

He never got off a second shot. The big Henry roared, and the man bucked in the saddle as if he were atop a bronco and then crumpled forward and toppled from the horse. Fargo ran forward as the young woman picked herself up from the ground, and in seconds she was clinging to him for a long moment, and he felt the warm softness of her breasts under the thin material of the nightgown. She pulled away and her doe brown eyes searched his face. "You were the one that spied on us and then got away," she said.

"In person," Fargo nodded.

"And somehow you were here to save my life," she said.

"Just happened by," Fargo said and she shook her head slowly.

"No, you came back and you were watching. But I don't understand. Why? Who are you?" she said.

"You first, honey," Fargo said.

She hesitated for a moment, and then her hand came out to touch his face. "All right, you saved my life. I cannot repay you for that, but I can tell you whatever you want to know about me," she said.

"That'd be a good start," Fargo said.

"But not here, with these *plebeyo* all over," she said. "We will talk as we ride back to my place."

"Just a minute," Fargo said as he strode to where the man lay on the ground, picked up his Colt, and tossed the old Remington away. The young woman climbed onto one of the horses and followed Fargo to where he had hidden the Ovaro.

"You called yourself Fargo," she said as he climbed onto the Ovaro. "Is that really your name?"

"It is," he said as he swung in beside her and they began the long ride back. "And your name?"

"Isabella Downing," she said. "My mother is Mexican. My father, who is dead, was American. My mother was actually born in Spain, a little town near Valencia."

"Where did Ed fit in?" Fargo questioned.

"Ed Cardon worked for my family for a long time. I trusted him, made him my right-hand man. It seems I misjudged him," she said with more sadness than anger, and Fargo felt her sidelong glance of appraisal. "It's plain you are not who I thought you might be, or you would have let them kill me," she said, giving voice to her thoughts.

"You mean they were from Vargas?" Fargo said and saw her eyes widen.

"Yes, from Vargas. But how do you know about Vargas?" Isabella asked.

"We'll get to that later. You're doing the telling now," Fargo said. "I was thinking you were part of Vargas's operation."

"Me, working for him? That *tacaño?* Never," the girl flared instantly.

"Then what were all those training maneuvers about?" Fargo asked. Her lips tightened, and she didn't answer. "You said you'd tell me whatever I want to know," he reminded her.

"I will, but not everything here. I want to wait till we return to the ranch. Painful things are not easy to talk about," she said.

"Fair enough," he said.

"But what about Skye Fargo? How do you come to ride into my world and save my life?" Isabella asked.

56

Fargo smiled back. "That can wait, too. I've things that are not easy to talk about."

She returned his smile. "Then let us ride," she said and put her horse into a fast canter. He caught up with her, rode hard alongside her, and admired the way she handled the horse, slender figure sitting the saddle with graceful ease, the top of the nightgown pressing hard against her breasts to outline the tiny points. When the dark buildings of the ranch finally came into sight, she led the way to the stable. "There are empty stalls. Choose one for that handsome Ovaro of yours," she said. She unsaddled her mount as he found a roomy corner stall for the pinto and soon walked to the main house with her. She lighted lamps in a large living room, richly furnished with leather sofas, wood-beamed high ceilings, Navajo rugs on the floor, and sturdy dark-wood cabinets against the walls. She went to one of the cabinets and drew out glasses and two bottles. "Mescal or tequila?" she asked.

"Tequila," he said, and she served the liquor with a small saucer of salt and folded herself beside him on one of the two sofas, drawing her legs up under her. The nightgown pulled tight to reveal the long curve of her breasts. He placed a dash of salt on his tongue, drank the tequila, then sat back.

"We have plenty of guest rooms. You may stay the night," Isabella said.

"Wouldn't mind a comfortable bed," Fargo said. "But it's time for talk now. Let's start with the men who paid Ed Cardon to bring you to them. Who were they?"

"They were from Vargas," Isabella said.

"Why did they want you dead?"

"He had to have told them about my plans," she said. "For his bag of money, of course."

"What plans?" Fargo asked. "Plans that had to do with all that training I watched?"

"Yes." She nodded. "I've been training a small group of men to rescue my mother. Rolando Vargas is holding her prisoner."

Fargo's brows lifted. "Why?" he asked.

"So he can force her to finance his army," Isabella said disdainfully, and Fargo felt his brows go higher.

"Your mother's financing Vargas's army?" he echoed with a frown.

Isabella nodded again. "My father made a lot of money in California in the shipping business. When he died, Mother inherited everything. She met Rolando Vargas a year after Father died. She needed attention. Father had always been too busy making money to be much of a lover. When Rolando Vargas came along with his smooth, Mexican charm, Mother was an easy mark for him. He played hard to get her to fall in love with him."

"You never liked him, I take it."

She made a scornful face. "He is am ambitious little weasel, a miserable *malvado*," she said. "I could never understand what my mother saw in him. When he suggested they go off together for a long trip, my mother was happy to agree, and the next thing I know she was his prisoner. I have not seen her since she left with him. I don't dare think of what he's doing to her to make her keep drawing money out for him."

"How do you know he's making her give him the money to finance his operation?" Fargo questioned.

"The bank in California sends its statements here," Isabella said, and Fargo finished his tequila. Suddenly, completely unexpectedly, he had found the answer to one of the main questions he'd come to explore. Isabella was becoming a beautiful gold mine of information, and he realized her words implied still more.

"You were training to rescue your mother. That means you must know where Vargas has his headquarters," Fargo said.

"Yes. I've watched his preparations for months, being very careful not to be caught. He feels so secure he doesn't even have sentries posted. I made mental notes of all the buildings and the wall around the main house where he's holding my mother."

"And built your own wall to practice scaling the real one when the time comes," Fargo said.

"Exactly." Isabella nodded.

"And practiced dry time runs for yourself," Fargo added, and she nodded again.

"Now it is your turn to tell me things," she said. "Why have you come here? How do you know about Rolando Vargas?"

"I was sent here," he said.

"Sent here?" Isabella frowned.

"By the President of the United States," Fargo said, and Isabella's face flooded with surprise. "You see, the government knows what Vargas wants to do, and they don't want him doing it. I was sent to find out everything I can and, if possible, stop him."

"My God, this is wonderful," Isabella said. "You have come to help me."

"Not so fast, honey," Fargo said. "I'm here to do a job. If that ties in with helping you, that's fine. If it doesn't, my job comes first."

"I can help you. We can help each other," Isabella said, excitement curling in her voice. "I will tell you everything I know about Vargas's plans, and you'll help me rescue my mother."

Fargo turned the offer over in his mind and

couldn't see anything wrong with it. "It's a deal, but you do things my way," he said.

She frowned at once. "What does that mean?"

"It means, for one thing, we don't go rushing in to try and get your mother out. Ed Cardon told them about your plans. They might be ready and waiting for you to try getting your mother. It's too big a risk, now."

She frowned at him. "All that training and preparation wasted," she muttered.

"Maybe not. We'll see. But we don't go barging in," he said.

Isabella's eyes searched his face again. "Why did they choose you to come here to find Vargas?" she asked.

"Because I'm called the Trailsman. I find trails where others do not. I make trails where others do not," he told her.

"Then you are a special man. That fits," she said with seriousness wreathing her face.

"How does it fit?" he asked.

"It fits your coming here, out of the blue, so to speak. Do you believe it fate, Fargo?"

"Maybe. I'm not sure. It seems to work sometimes," he said.

"This is one of those times. I know it. I feel it inside," she said, rising and moving to stand before him. "You appeared and saved my life. That was the first sign." Her arms flew around his neck, and her lips were on his, a fleeting kiss, yet made of sweet fire, and then she drew back and looked apologetic. "I'm sorry. I get excited too easily," she said.

"I've nothing against that," he told her and, scanning her lovely face, decided she was a strange mixture of strength and softness, womanly determination and wide-eyed naïveté.

"There is more to talk about, but I am very tired. Let us do it in the morning," she said, suddenly sounding depleted. "I'll show you to your room."

"I'll get my things," he said, hurried from the house to the stable, and came back with his travel pouch. Isabella led him to a bedroom down a wide corridor where a large bed took up much of a room that was tastefully hung with drapes and furnished with an oak dresser.

"Have a good night's sleep," she said. "Find your way to the kitchen in the morning. Breakfast will be there. I will, also." She paused at the doorway, dark brown eyes shining. "I feel so good about everything suddenly. I have a new confidence," she said.

"Hang onto it," he told her as she left, and he began to shed clothes, his lips turning grim. Her new confidence was perhaps unwarranted. She had worked hard to prepare to rescue her mother, but that might indicate more hope than realism, he muttered to himself. Yet, if he could find a way to rescue her mother, he could, with one stroke, also put an end to Vargas's funds—and perhaps to his entire adventure. But it wouldn't be done Isabella's way, not anymore. He'd have to come up with a different approach. But he was too tired to concentrate, and he let sleep hold the thought for him.

5

When morning came, he found his way to the kitchen, where Isabella waited. But she was not alone. Some dozen men lined up behind her in a half circle and a handful of women interspersed. He recognized a few from the training maneuvers he'd watched, and Isabella, dressed in a white blouse that set off her black hair and eyebrows, smiled at him, excitement flashing in her dark eyes. "This is my little army, Fargo. Everyone has been trained to do a special task," she said. "They have all worked here at the ranch for a long time, and they are loyal."

"That's what you thought about Ed Cardon," he half whispered, and her lips grew tight for a moment.

"I've told them how you have come to help us and how you already saved my life. I've also told them I will listen to your advice and you are against going after my mother now. Naturally, they are disappointed after all our work and training," Isabella said.

Fargo's gaze swept the small gathering. They looked back at him, every face serious. Most of the men were between thirty and forty years of age, he guessed. "You may have your chance. All your work wasn't for nothing," he told them and saw their faces brighten. Isabella introduced each one individually, and Fargo made no attempt to remember names. After they all filed out of the kitchen, he was left alone with Isabella who served him a cup of strong, bracing coffee. "Very good," he commented. "What is it?"

"Mexican coatepec," she said. "Have you thought of another way of rescuing my mother?"

"Not yet. By the way, what's her name?" he asked.

"Celia," Isabella said.

"If you managed to get her out of Vargas's place, how did you expect to get away. You know he'd be coming after you."

"Of course, but we were prepared to outrun him. We knew that sooner or later, in this hot, dry country, his men and horses would have to turn back for water."

"Wouldn't you face the same problem?" Fargo queried.

She smiled smugly and went to a cabinet to return with a rolled map she spread out in front of him on the table. He saw where it had been marked with circles in various places. "We mapped out the location of every *tinajas* in southern Arizona," she said.

"What are *tinajas*?" Fargo asked.

"They are the natural waterholes that store rainwater. Some hold only a little. Some hold a lot. Most people only know the *tinajas* near where they live. With this map we will be able to keep going when he has to turn back."

"I'm impressed," Fargo said honestly. "This map may still come in handy." She returned the map to the cabinet as he finished the coffee and rose to his feet. "I want to have a look at Vargas's operation. How do I find it?"

"I'll take you," she said and saw the moment's

hesitation that crossed his face. "It is my mother, my fight. I won't be left out, Fargo," she said.

"Understood." He nodded, and she linked her arm in his as she walked out of the house with him.

"Besides, with you here I feel so confident about everything," Isabella said, and Fargo shot her a quick glance. There was no attempt to bolster him, he saw, no gratuitous gaiety in her. She was absolutely sincere, dark eyes shining happily. He'd not dim her optimism, he decided. Perhaps he could borrow some, and he smiled inwardly.

When they had the horses saddled, she led the way directly south toward the border, staying near the base of the Growler Mountains. He rode beside her, and she didn't hurry her horse in the burning sun, passing through long stretches of jojoba where he glimpsed wild cattle grazing on the shrubs in the distance. He saw the signs, mostly spoor, of coyote, and prairie falcons swept overhead with graceful effortlessness. He paused to watch a herd of javelina pass near, snorting and shuffling, looking not unlike some strange mixture of a pig and a tapir, their blunt, flat snouts sweeping up cholla as if the plant had no spines. Even from a distance he could smell the musky odor of the javelina herd, hardly a perfume, yet not entirely unpleasant.

"How much farther," he asked Isabella as they rode downward through a rocky draw.

"Soon," she said, and his eyes went to the expanse of dark and scrungy bushes they rode through, a growth unfamiliar to him.

"What do you call these?" he asked.

"Limber bush," she said. "The Mexicans call them *sangre de drago*, blood of the dragon. They call them that because they have a red sap the Indians often use as a dye. The Indians, the Papago and the Maricopa and the Apache, as well, have another name for them. They called limber bush the hiding plant because they can crawl through it for miles without being seen. It grows thick enough and just tall enough to hide someone." She paused, a half smile touching her wide mouth. "Limber bush grows all the way down to Vargas's compound," she said and spurred her cinder gray horse forward. He caught up to her as she went over a stony ridge and into a stand of juniper that lasted long enough to bring them out onto a ledge where, in the distance, he saw the sprawling compound. The land led downward, at one side through a series of narrow crevices in a rocky decline, on the other side a wide slope thickly covered by limber bush.

He chose the narrow crevices and Isabella followed as he rode closer to the collection of houses. He halted at a place that let him see the entire spread below, and Isabella squeezed her horse alongside him. A white clay wall surrounded the main house, and he smiled with a glance at Isabella, then let his eyes sweep the rest of the sprawling compound. He counted at least fifteen buildings, barracks, supply sheds, storage buildings, stables, wagon barns, and corrals filled with horses that stretched out beyond. At least four squads of men were training, using the sabre, the sword, rifle maneuvers, hand-to-hand combat, and at one side, target practice. Eyes narrowed, he finally spoke to Isabella without taking his gaze from the scene below.

"I make a rough count of a hundred men down there. He can't think he'll take on the Mexican army with a hundred men, not even a division. It'd be suicide," Fargo said.

"I thought about that, too. But I've never seen more than a hundred men training," Isabella said.

"But maybe not the same hundred," Fargo said, and she frowned at him.

"I never thought of that," she admitted, and Fargo's eyes studied a long building where barrels were lined up in double rows against one wall.

"I'd guess those are grain barrels," he said.

"Probably. That seems to be a food storehouse. I've seen sacks of potatoes and sides of dried beef, bags of squash and corn put inside, a lot more than a hundred men would need," Isabella said, and Fargo's eyes shifted to the long line of Owensboro seed-bed wagons. They weren't designed for troop transport, but they could well be used to carry food. "Let's assume he has a lot more men," Fargo said. "Where are they? Where the hell could he hide them?"

"I don't know," Isabella said. "But my people have heard the men he's recruiting are mostly mercenaries from California and Texas. He also has many Mexicans, men who want to see Juarez ousted and a new government put in place. Many of these, I hear, are men who fought against Juarez's taking over and cannot go back to Mexico so long as he is there."

"And all I see is a hundred men," Fargo muttered. "It doesn't fit. There have to be more, someplace, somewhere." He had just cast a glance skyward to see the sun beginning to move toward the horizon when a door in one of the larger buildings opened and a dozen horsemen came out, riding in twos, each carrying a rifle. The front gate of the compound was opened for them, and they rode at a steady trot and began to climb into the hills.

"Where are they going?" Isabella questioned.

"They're an escort if I ever saw one," Fargo said. "I'd say they're on their way to meet someone or something. I think we ought to follow and find out."

"Let's go," Isabella said, but his hand came out to rest on her arm.

"Easy," he said. "We don't have to follow too closely. They'll be easy enough to hear." She nodded, and they waited till the last of the dozen riders were out of sight before backing their horses out of the narrow passageway. Fargo followed a distance behind even as the dusk came and turned into night. The sound of the dozen riders was easy to pick up in the dry, rock-filled land. The riders continued on until the moon rose high, and Fargo heard Isabella's whispered remark.

"I'd say they were heading for the San Cristobal Wash which is on the other side of these hills," she said.

"Why do you say that?" Fargo asked.

"Because it comes down from the Gila River, and anything coming in from California usually follows the Gila River," Isabella explained. Fargo nodded in understanding and held up one hand and reined the Ovaro to a halt.

"They've stopped, up ahead somewhere," he said, his head cocked to one side as he listened. "I hear rein chains rattling. They're going to bed down for the rest of the night." He swung to the ground, and Isabella did the same and followed him as he led the Ovaro up a side path in the mostly stone mountain formations to where a cluster of junipers grew on the side of a tall rock. Soft, almost grassy shrubs lined the base of the junipers, and he halted. "We'll bed down here. They can't see us from below," he said. "I've an extra blanket if you need it."

"Thanks, I've a double-sheet in my saddlebag," Isabella said, and after unsaddling her horse, she disappeared into the junipers. Fargo undressed, tossed a towel over his groin, and lay down on his bedroll. When Isabella reappeared, she had the sheet wrapped around her, leaving beautifully rounded shoulders bare. She settled herself near Fargo, and he saw her eyes move across the smoothly muscled tanness of his torso. She pulled her gaze away and settled down in her sheet. "Good night, Fargo," she said softly. "I'm glad you are here."

"I'm glad you're glad," he said. "Now get some sleep." He pulled sleep around himself and shut out the sound of kangeroo rats and night lizards. When he woke, the morning sun had begun to slide over the distant tops of the Castle Dome Mountains and Isabella lay on her side, part of the sheet pulled down enough to reveal the long, lovely curve of one breast, smooth, pale olive skin that seemed to shimmer. She woke, perhaps subconsciously feeling his gaze, turned lazily, and the long, lovely curve was swallowed up by the sheet. She gathered herself in the sheet, took her canteen, and disappeared behind the junipers. He was dressed when she returned, and as he saddled the Ovaro, he watched her take a brush from her saddlebag and stroke her long, thick, black hair with it, making the simple act thoroughly sensual—but with no attempt to do so, everything perfectly natural for her.

Finally, she sat the cinder gray horse beside him, and Fargo started down the rock-strewn slope. Soon they once again followed the sound of the riders in front of them. The sun burned down with withering force, and he watched an iguana on a rock, completely impervious to the scorching rays. The riders ahead halted often to rest, and Fargo was grateful for small favors. Noon had passed when he saw the deep ravines of the San Cristobal Wash stretch out before him. The dozen riders were small shapes in the distance, moving along the dry wash, and he hung back still further until the shapes disappeared. Moving forward, Fargo stayed with the wash and saw perspiration coating Isabella's shirt, making it cling to her, outlining the curve of her breasts. It was the only softly beautiful sight in this hot, arid, forbidding land, he decided.

The dryness of the wash suddenly became less so, and he saw traces of water on the bed. The traces became spreading wetness, then actually shallow water. They were nearing the Gila River, and they rode the last part of the wash in ankle deep water. The river stretched out before them as the day passed into midafternoon and the land flattened, the long ribbon of water sparkling in the sun. The riders had turned west, and Fargo led the way up a slope that became high rock of ancient lava formations and let him look down at the river. He increased his pace and held it until the dozen riders appeared alongside the riverbank. They drew to a halt, and Fargo reined in, peering west where the line of wagons approached. They reached the dozen riders, a single driver for each wagon, and Fargo saw they were mostly Owensboro cut-under haulage wagons, each pulled by a two-horse team. Fargo's eyes moved across the contents of each wagon, starting with the long, narrow boxes that filled the first two, the canvas-covered crates in others, and the two wagons loaded with barrels.

"Boxes of rifles, crates of handguns, ammunition, gunpowder, maybe some dynamite, enough for more than a hundred men," Fargo said. "And he's probably expecting another shipment, which means he must have the bulk of his army hidden away somewhere." He fell silent and watched the dozen riders form an escort around the line of wagons as they rolled forward under a sun that had started to dip below the mountains. Fargo stayed in place as the wagons rolled on, finally turning down into the San Cristobal Draw as darkness approached. When Fargo followed, carefully staying on the higher land with Isabella, he found the wagons had formed a double row to camp for the night.

"What are you thinking?" Isabella asked, watching his eyes stay narrowed as he scanned the scene.

"I'm thinking that if Vargas didn't get that shipment, it'd really set him back with whatever timetable he's on," Fargo said as Isabella's eyes widened.

"But there's no way the two of us can stop that shipment," she said. "Look, they've posted sentries."

"I see that." Fargo nodded. "But I see something else," he said with a grim smile. "I see an awful lot of gunpowder just waiting to be exploded."

"No, you couldn't get to it," Isabella said. "Maybe if they didn't have sentries, but not this way."

"They won't make it any easier," Fargo conceded. "But I've dealt with sentries before, especially this kind." Isabella frowned back. "Amateurs," he said. "After a few hours they're half asleep standing up." He led the way farther down the rocks to finally halt only a few feet above the bed of the dry wash, dismounted, and settled down to wait. Isabella came to sit close against him.

"I don't want you to do this," she said. "I don't want you to get yourself killed for this one shipment."

"You want a better reason," Fargo said blandly and saw the color rush into her cheeks.

"I didn't mean it to sound that way, but, in a way, yes," she said. "One must choose what to live for and one must choose what to die for. They must both be important."

"This is important enough, trust me," he said, and she settled back, her arm touching his. He let the hours slide by, and when the moon reached the midnight sky, he rose and began to rummage through his saddlebag.

"What are you looking for?" Isabella asked.

"Matches. I thought I had some in here."

"I have some," Isabella said and went to her horse to return with four matches, the long, slender kind generally called lucifers. He pushed them into his pocket and met Isabella's grave gaze. "I can't just sit here and do nothing," she said.,

"You're not. You're my support. If you hear a shot, that'll mean it's gone wrong. You come a-charging with the horses," he said, and she held his hand for a moment longer before he moved away down the rocky slope. When he reached the flat bed of the wash, he paused and drew the double-edged blade from his calf-holster, dropped to his stomach, and began to crawl toward the double line of wagons. Six of the escort stood sentry, two at one side of the wagons, two at the other, a fifth man up in front, and the sixth at the rear. Fargo moved slowly across the dry stone bed toward the sixth sentry, inching his way forward, the dark shadows his only cover. He halted, his eyes sweeping the wagons. The two wagons carrying the powder kegs were in the center, and he swore softly to himself. He brought his gaze to the sentry at the rear of the wagons and inched his way forward again. The man leaned back against the tailgate of one of the Owensboros, only half awake, Fargo saw, and he risked crawling another two feet closer.

The sentry leaned his head back against the tailgate, and Fargo brought his right arm forward, the throwing knife in his hand. He pushed himself upward to his knees and, with a sweeping, quick motion, sent the slender blade hurtling through the air. He was on his feet, loping forward in a crouch as the knife slammed into the man's chest, embedding itself to the hilt. Fargo reached the figure as it slowly crumpled in time to catch it before it hit the ground. He lowered the figure silently to the ground, pulled the blade free, and wiped it clean on the man's shirt. He kept hold of it as he dragged the figure under the wagon and left it there.

On his hands and knees he began to move beneath the line of wagons until he reached one holding the barrels of gunpowder. He allowed himself a grim smile as all he had counted on came true. The floor of the old wagon held long open cracks where the old floorboards no longer fitted tightly together, and he halted beneath the widest of the cracks. One of the gunpowder barrels rested directly over it, and settling himself on one knee, he began to cut into the bottom of the barrel, short, jabbing motions that at first dislodged only a thin trickle of wood dust and then, as he worked the hole deeper and wider, the little chips of wood began to fall. It was cramped, straining labor and he paused often to rest his wrist, listening to the muttered sounds of the sentries on either side of him. It seemed an endless amount of time as he forced himself to work slowly and silently, digging with the point of the blade, turning, twisting, carving out one tiny piece of wood after another and then, he didn't know how long after, the blade thrust upward through the small hole he'd made in the barrel.

He pulled his hat off and held it under the hole, drew the knife out, and watched the slow stream of gunpowder pour down to finally fill his hat. He moved from the hole and began to crawl forward under the wagons, pouring a trail of the gunpowder from his hat as he went. He could see the boots of the sentries not more than a dozen inches from where he crawled, and he inched himself forward with the silence of a serpent. When he reached the front wagon with his trail of gunpowder, he halted, peered under the hickory axle and shafts, and saw the legs of the forward sentry. Carefully turning himself around under the wagon, Fargo began to crawl back alongside the trail of gunpowder he'd lain.

Passing the barrel with the hole he'd fashioned, he saw the small triangular mound of gunpowder still accumulating. He crawled on, again laying a trail of the powder under the wagons at the rear, and his hat was empty when he reached the slain sentry under the last wagon. He slid out from under the wagon, lifted himself to one knee, and lighted one of the matches. He laid the burning match alongside the trail of gunpowder, pushed himself to his feet, and began streaking across the ground with every ounce of speed his powerful legs could muster. The match would take perhaps another three seconds to ignite the gunpowder, which would flare up, sizzling as it did, for perhaps another ten seconds before it reached the mound of gunpowder in the center of the wagons. The explosion would be tremendous, he knew, and he paid no attention to the shouts he heard from behind as the other sentries spotted his racing figure. Only two rifle shots cut through the night as he flung himself into the air in a leaping dive against the base of the shallow slope.

The explosion erupted as he hit the ground, a deafening roar, and he turned to look back at the wagons where a brilliant sheet of yellow-orange light flew upward. The dynamite went in another three seconds, as did the boxes of ammunition, and the night became a series of exploding balls of flame and bits and pieces of wagon spiraling skyward in all directions. A burning wheel landed not more than a dozen feet from him, and he instinctively ducked and rolled away. Sweeping the scene with his eyes again, he saw more than pieces of wagon strewn about and watched the brilliant yellow-orange begin to diminish, turn to dull red and finally into a pall of gray smoke that lay over everything, interspersed only by pieces of wagon still burning.

He rose to his feet, stepped back from the base of the slope, and waved both arms in the direction of where he'd left Isabella. It was only moments before he saw the two horses racing down the slope toward him, and when she drew to a halt, she leaped from the saddle and buried herself into his chest, clinging to him with both arms. "God, I was so afraid you'd been caught in the explosion. I thought I saw someone running, but I wasn't sure it was you," she said, and he held her and felt her trembling until finally she stopped.

Her dark eyes were still full of concern as she looked up at him, and he grinned down at her. "A little closer than I wanted, but close doesn't count," he said.

"You are marvelous, *maravilloso*, Fargo. I think perhaps you can do anything," she said.

"Almost anything." He laughed. "Now let's get out of here. It'll be daybreak in an hour."

"We've been up all night. I'm too tired to ride all the way back in the day's heat," she said.

"Wasn't figuring to," Fargo told her. "We'll put some distance between us and this place. When the shipment doesn't arrive, Vargas will send men out looking for it." He climbed into the saddle and led the way out of the wash where the gray cloud still hung over the scene, its own shroud. He rode higher, away from the wash, into the hills, and as dawn began to break, he found a slope where a thick stand of ajo oak and piñon pine rose skyward. Nosing into the interior of the trees where the branches were so thick the direct sun wouldn't penetrate, he found a spot to bed down, and after they unsaddled the horses, Isabella took her sheet and disappeared again for a moment.

He lay on his bedroll, naked except for a towel, when she returned wrapped in the sheet, and she lay down close to him, staying on one elbow for a moment as her eyes traveled across his muscled torso. "Gallant, brave, and handsome, you are like the knights of old," she said. "They were all rare men, exceptional men. They had to be to become knights. You would have been one, had you lived then."

Fargo laughed. "You think so?"

"Oh, yes. You are one now, without the armor," Isabella said, and he saw she was being completely serious, her dark eyes deep and wide. "Are you going to tell me I'm a romantic?" she asked.

"The thought crossed my mind," he said.

"Others have said that. I guess I am. I'm glad to be a romantic. To be a romantic is to believe in good overcoming evil, to believe there are things that are pure and true. I guess being a romantic is to believe in love and the power of love. Not too many people do that nowadays."

"Different times, different attitudes," Fargo said.

She gave him a small, half shy smile. "Not everyone. There are those who still believe in honor, trust, fidelity, chivalry. You do, too."

"How do you know that?" He smiled.

"Because of all the things you've done. Because you're here," she said with simple logic.

"I'm here because I was sent to do a job," he told

her gently, and she smiled again, a hint of smug wisdom in it.

"Nothing is ever as it seems," she said.

"You read a lot about those old days of knights and fair maidens?" he asked.

"Oh, yes, since I was a little girl. I read everything I could, not only about the Knights of the Round Table, King Arthur, and Sir Lancelot, but the great knights of Spanish culture, El Cid and Cervantes's Don Quixote. I especially liked Don Quixote. Others laughed at him, made fun of him, but he was still a knight because he believed in all the good things, and that's what counts, what you believe in."

"I believe in getting some sleep," he said, and she stretched down beside him.

"Yes, indeed," she said, and he watched as she closed her eyes, breasts pushing up the sheet in a lovely curve. She was indeed a strange mixture, he decided, childlike romantic and determined young woman, soft and warm and sweetly impulsive, yet with the steel to prepare an armed assault, sentimental idealist and hard realist. It was a mixture that made her two people in one and both fascinating. He watched her sleep for a few minutes longer, her breasts under the sheet rising and falling with rhythmic loveliness, and then he closed his eyes and let tiredness sweep him away.

6

Fargo woke near noon, but the direct sun still didn't filter through the trees. The little spot was a cool oasis from the broiling sun outside, and he saw Isabella wake and push to her feet, keeping the sheet around her and go to her saddlebag as he pulled on trousers. When she returned, she held her canteen and in her palm two small, dried pieces of what looked to him like yellowish cubes. "Take one," she said. "Put it into your mouth and then take a mouthful from the canteen. Watch me." She popped one cube into her mouth, drank from the canteen and swished the water inside her mouth, gargled with it, and finally spit it out. He did the same and knew surprise touched his face as, after a moment, he felt a sweet, refreshing taste in his mouth that grew stronger, more invigorating. He gargled, as Isabella had done, and the clean taste stayed after he spit out the water.

"Great," he breathed. "What was it?"

"The pulp of the barrel cactus, boiled in sugar syrup and dried," she said. "That's why the barrel cactus is called candy cactus by the natives." She lay back, the sheet still firmly around her and, enclosed in its folds, still managed to look seductive as she stretched her arms upward and the top of the sheet dropped enough to show the swelling curves of both breasts. "I know we have to go, but it's so nice here. It makes me almost want to forget about rescuing my mother and just stay here," she said and lowered her arms as she closed her eyes. "This country is that way, you know," she went on with her eyes shut. "Dry and arid and hard and unyielding, then suddenly there are places of absolute beauty. They always take you by surprise, like the beautiful red blossoms of a buckhorn cholla."

"I think you are one of those places, beauty that takes you by surprise," Fargo said. She smiled, eyes still closed.

"Gallantry, another quality of a true knight," she said.

Fargo's eyes suddenly narrowed as he caught the movement almost directly behind her head, and the silent, sliding form of the snake drew closer. A big diamondback rattler, he saw as his hand moved slowly toward the Colt in the holster nearby. The snake was moving closer to Isabella, only inches away from her now, but Fargo kept his hand slow. It took damn little to make a rattler strike, a sudden motion, a sound. They were always nervous. He kept his voice soft and low as he spoke.

"Don't move, Isabella," he said. "Don't move." He saw her eyes snap open, fright instant in them. "Don't move," he repeated. "Don't talk. Don't breathe." He slid the Colt out of the holster, slowly brought it up as the rattler began to lift its head, its forked tongue darting out, drawing in the message of warm flesh. Fargo took aim and swore to himself. The bullet would have to pass over Isabella's arm with not the space of a sheet of paper between it and her skin. The snake rose a fraction of an inch higher, and Fargo's finger tightened on the trigger, aware that he couldn't risk waiting for a better moment. The serpent's tongue was still darting out, faster now, as the bullet smashed into its head, sending the coils lashing into the air, a physical reaction as its head blew away.

Isabella screamed as she rolled toward him, still wrapped in the sheet, and he caught her, stopped her, and rested one hand on her trembling body. He could feel the warmth of her under the sheet. "It's over," he said as he rose, stepped across her, and picked up the remains of the rattler and tossed it down the slope. He turned, then dropped to his knees beside her, and she sat up, came against him, and he felt the tips of her breasts pressing into his chest, his hands against her naked back. She clung to him, pressing her nakedness into him, all softness, her skin velvet smooth. She lifted herself up further, and her face drew back, dark eyes peering at him.

"Again," she murmured. "Once again." Her lips came to his and held there, sweet softness. "You have come for me. I have been here for you," she said. "It was to be." Her lips pressed harder against his, then opened, and he felt the tip of her tongue, only for an instant, and then she drew it back. The brown eyes were wide as she lay back on the bedroll with him, and her hands fell from his shoulders. The sheet slipped entirely from her, and on his knees before her, Fargo took in her loveliness, slender body of pale olive skin, breasts beautifully cupped with rosy pink nipples, a long waist and narrow hips, almost concave little belly, and a triangle as jet black as the hair that framed her face. Long, slender legs, held tightly together, stretched out, and he caught the faint tremor that coursed through her body as he touched the tip of his finger to one rosy pink nipple. Shedding trousers, he pressed his body gently against hers. "Oh, oh God . . . oh," Isabella breathed, responding to the touch of flesh to flesh, and he moved his chest back and forth across the small nipples.

She gasped out in pleasure, and her hands dug into his sides as he brought his lips down upon one smooth, pale olive breast, sucked on it, drew it into his mouth, and felt the tip rub against his tongue. Isabella made a long, low, moaning sound, and he let his tongue circle the small tip and felt the tiny protrusion fill out and grow firmer as more tiny tremors went through her again. "Yes, yes . . . oh, yes, so good, so good," she murmured. He moved one hand down her body and caressed the little indention in the almost concave belly. Pulling his mouth from her breast, he let his lips trace along the same path his hand had explored, and Isabella's hands clutched at his shoulders as she moaned.

His hand moved downward again, across the velvet pale olive skin, pressed down again into the jet black triangle, his fingers pushing through the soft-wire nap, and he felt the swell of her Venus mound. Isabella made murmuring sounds, and her hips twisted to one side, then the other, and he heard the gasped catch in her voice as his hand slipped down farther to rest at the point of the jet triangle. Her slender legs were still held together, he glimpsed, and he let his hand move down along one smooth top, then stroked gently, and she moaned though her legs stayed tight. He brought his hand back up the point of the black triangle, rested against the curling tendrils that strayed outward, and suddenly he felt the touch of warm moistness.

He let his hand gently press down between her thighs, ever so gently,. Isabella's legs moved, grew less tight, and he rested his hand between the warm thighs, right under the dark portal. He moved slowly with firm gentleness, and again he felt her legs relax, her thighs half offer themselves. He shifted his body, let his mouth caress one cupped breast as his hand slid slowly upward, paused, and rested against the soft threshold. "Oh, my God . . . oh, yes, oh, yes, yes . . ." Isabella mouthed, her voice hardly more than a whisper, and Fargo touched the roseate lips, moved deeper, and felt the flow of her rush forth in the eternal welcome. Isabella's whisper became a low moan, the low moan an undulating murmur, and when he brought his eager member over to rest upon the jet triangle, she gave a half scream as her fingers tightened against his back.

He felt the slender legs straighten, part, knees suddenly lift, coming up to rest against his buttocks, then fall aside, and her thighs came around his waist, a moist, warm embrace. Her pelvis was moving, slow upward surges as tiny sounds came from her, and he slid downward, letting his throbbing eagerness slip into her. Isabella screamed at the touch, all the overwhelming ecstasy of sensation engulfing her, all her wanting contained in that single scream. Her hands clawed down his back as she surged her pelvis upward to meet his penetrating thrusts, and he felt her tightness surrounding him, an encompassing vise of rapture. She cried out now with each surge of her pelvis, each cry an entreaty and a promise, and tiny clusters of words found their way through her cries: "Yes, yes, good . . . so good, so nice . . . oh, God, more, oh more."

He lay with her, wanting only to join in the absolute ecstasy she exhibited, and he saw her neck arch backward, her long-waisted, slender body twist and turn and the brown eyes now on fire with a dark brilliance. Tiny drops of perspiration suddenly coated the pale olive skin and added another dimension of glossy sensuality to her. Isabella reached arms up, drew him down against her, and pressed his mouth onto one beautifully cupped breast as her body surged upward against his, and he saw the black halo of hair tossing from one side to the other. "Yes, Fargo . . . oh, *mia dia*, yes . . . more, more . . . oh, more," she half whispered against the side of his face, and he continued to move with slow steadiness inside her. The slender legs fell apart for a moment, then came back to tighten against him again. She was all slow fire, a body made of sensual writhings, and suddenly he felt her upward thrusts grow longer, harsher, her pubic mound hitting against his groin, holding there, then falling away, and surging against him again, and again, and again.

"I . . . it is happening, oh, God, Fargo, it is happening," she said, and he heard the pleasure and triumph in her cry and felt a certain sense of relief as he became aware he could not have held back for much longer. She thrust against him, clung to him with arms and legs wrapped around his body, and he felt her vibrating, quivering with a tremendous intensity, all her gasps and cries turned inward as the soundless flesh spoke with tactile delight. When her slender form finally ceased its ferocious vibrating, she went limp, legs falling from his sides, arms sliding from his back. He stayed atop her, staying inside her, still throbbing. "Yes, oh yes . . . so nice, so nice," Isabella murmured, her eyes closed, and when she opened the dark pupils, he saw her searching his face, and she winced when he drew from her but more with disappointment than pain.

He lay beside her, enjoying the slender, pale olive beauty of her, a body sensual in its every curve, yet strangely virginal in its freshness. The flesh echoing the admixture of the spirit, he commented silently. Isabella turned, pushed onto one elbow, and leaned forward, embracing him as she pressed warm, smooth nakedness against him.

"It was meant to be, all of it," she said, and he frowned at her. "You coming here, I waiting here, you bringing yourself to me, I giving myself to you, all meant to be. We are one now, part of each other. You are my Don Quixote, though you are no Knight of the Woeful Countenance. You are my knight of the handsome countenance." Her little laugh was musical, and she hugged him to her again. "I will be faithful to you, Fargo. We will be faithful to each other, the way it is meant to be."

"Sure thing, honey. Meanwhile, there are a lot more things that need doing here and now. Let's get moving," he said, and she swung herself away, a graceful motion that made her breasts sway in unison, and he hurriedly pulled on clothes before his resolve to leave gave way. They rode back along the high sides of the wash of San Cristobel, turned away from it by midafternoon, and reached Isabella's place as dusk began to dim the land. The others rushed out to greet Isabella with anxious relief, and she promised to tell them why they'd taken so long to return. "After a hot meal," she said, and when Fargo stabled the Ovaro, he returned to the house to find Isabella waiting in the dining room, a fragrant dish of chicken and rice on the table.

"Have you thought of a way to rescue my mother?" Isabella asked as they ate.

"No, but I've thought about how to maybe find a way," Fargo said. "I'm going to pay Vargas a visit tomorrow."

Isabella almost dropped her fork as she stared at him. "He'll never let you leave," she said.

"Yes, he will," Fargo said. "That's why blowing

up the ammunition shipment was so important. He'll be even more interested in talking to me."

"I'm not sure I understand." Isabella frowned.

"You will when I come back," he said.

"It is crazy. He won't even see you. He'll just have you shot," Isabella insisted.

"No, he won't," Fargo said. "While I'm inside, I'll find out where he's holding your mother."

"Somewhere in the main house. I caught a glimpse of her just outside it one day. He has to keep her fed and well so she can sign the withdrawal notices to the bank," Isabella said.

"Then I'll find out exactly where in the main house," Fargo said.

"I'm afraid for you to go there," Isabella said, and a half pout slid across her face.

"Don't be," he assured her, but the pout stayed as she cleared away the dishes.

"The others are waiting for me," she said. "Will you wait?"

"No, I'm going to bed. We'll talk in the morning," he said, and she hurried away with a nod. He rose and went to the big bedroom and shed clothes at once, realizing he was still tired. He lay awake for a spell in the large bed, sorting out his plans for the coming day, and he'd just closed off further thoughts when he heard the door open. He half rose, one hand automatically moving toward the Colt hanging on the bedpost, when he saw the nightgowned figure coming toward him, a silver white form in the near darkness. "I said we could talk in the morning," he reminded her.

"'I didn't come to talk," Isabella said as she lowered herself to the bed, and suddenly the nightgown was dropping from her shoulders. True to her words, she turned the night into a time of pure sensuality, again making love with a wonderful eagerness that was rewarding in its guileless openness. When she finally lay pressed against him and asleep, it was with the trusting and caring contentment of a child. But a little before dawn she woke, the very practical, realistic side of her in charge. "I must go. It would not be right for the others to know I was here," she said and swept up the nightgown as she crossed the room in quick steps, her thin rear hardly jouncing. Fargo returned to sleep for another few hours and when he woke, washed and dressed. Isabella waited for him in the kitchen with another bracing cup of the *coatepec*.

"I'm sure he won't let you see my mother, but if you should, tell her help is on the way," Isabella said.

"I'll try," Fargo told her. "I'll be back tonight, but if I'm not, don't go getting upset. If I'm asked to stay overnight, I'll do it."

"When do I start getting upset?" she asked.

"If I'm not back in a couple of days," he said. She went to the stable with him and kissed him after he had the Ovaro saddled and ready to go.

"Be careful, my love," she said as he rode away. He would ordinarily have been rankled by her words. He'd always disliked possessive women. But there was none of that in her, only an honest, wide-eyed caring, almost a kind of hero-worship, he realized. He'd sit her down for a long talk one day and invoke that hard realist he knew was also in her. But now he turned his thoughts and the Ovaro south to Rolando Vargas's compound. At midafternoon he reached the sprawling collection of buildings, and he leaned down and removed the note from the pocket inside his boot and pushed it into his shirt pocket.

He nosed the pinto from the rocks and down to the dry flat land, then kept the horse at a steady walk under the hot sun as he approached the compound. He was almost at the front gate when three riders came out to meet him, all armed with carbines. One was a Mexican, dark olive skin and south-of-the-border features, the other two rough-looking Anglos. "What are you doing here, mister?" one of the white men asked in a gravelly voice.

"Came to see Rolando Vargas," Fargo said calmly.

The man uttered a wry snort. "Just like that?" he said, and Fargo nodded. "The general doesn't see every sodbuster who shows up. Now, if you're looking to join up, we'll take you to see Henry Arons."

"I'm looking to see Vargas, and he'll see me," Fargo said and pulled the note from his pocket. "Got a letter of introduction, you might say."

"We'll take it," the man said, but Fargo pulled his hand back.

"Sorry. It's for Vargas, personal delivery," Fargo said, and the three men exchanged quick glances.

"The general's got an assistant," the man said. "That's the best we can do."

"It's a start," Fargo said and followed the three men into the compound, his eyes sweeping the scene. Three squads were training in a distant field, and Fargo saw bags of potatoes being carried into the food storage barn from a cotton-bed wagon. His gaze paused at a low-roofed building to one side where three guards stood at attention, each carrying a rifle. The men led him to the main building, a beautiful example of classic Spanish architecture, the whitewashed stone wall surrounding it, and through the open iron gate he saw the graceful wings of the house that stretched on either side from the arched, almost monasterylike center section.

The three riders dismounted in front of the

house, and the one man beckoned Fargo to follow him in, leading the way down a thickly carpeted corridor hung with rich drapes. He paused at an open doorway. "Man here says he's got a letter for the general," he said, waited, and then turned to Fargo. "Go on in," he said, and Fargo walked past him into a large room, richly furnished with a heavy walnut desk in the center, walls of paneled, dark wood, and tall, arched windows. Two large sofas faced the desk and the figure behind it, and Fargo felt shocked surprise flood his face. It was as if he were staring at a slightly askew version of Isabella, the face a little coarser, cheekbones a trifle heavier, eyes blacker, a handsome face with more surface strength in it than Isabella's. His eyes went to the rest of her and saw a body a little heavier than Isabella's, breasts deeper, curves rounder under a deep-green dress, but the overall likeness was nonetheless astonishing.

His initial surprise at her likeness to Isabella was matched by his surprise at her presence, a woman very much in command. If she were a prisoner, a woman held against her will, she surely was the most assured, cool, and contained one he'd ever seen. He'd walk very carefully, he quickly decided as her black eyes surveyed him. "What's this all about, mister?" she asked. Fargo handed her the letter and watched the frown slide across her brow as she read it. Her shining, black eyes returned to him when she finished, searching his face with frank approval. She put the letter on the desk, then rang a small bell, and a man appeared in the doorway. "Get the general. He's watching the training in sector four," she said, and as the man vanished, she scanned the brief note again and brought her shining, black eyes back to Fargo. "Well, Mister Skye

Fargo, I am surprised, to say the least. I'm sure the general will be, too."

"I guess that's natural enough. I was told you're the general's assistant. That makes two of us surprised. Didn't expect a woman," Fargo said.

"I'm more than the general's assistant," she said, the implication clear. "I'll be his wife soon."

Fargo nodded as he wondered if Isabella had any idea of all of this. "Then you must be Celia Downing," he said, and it was the woman's turn to raise her eyebrows in surprise.

"How did you know that?" she questioned.

"It's my business to know things. Besides, Washington gave me a pretty good briefing on the general. Your name came up," Fargo said. He had already decided not to mention Isabella yet and was content to let Celia Downing carefully take him in from head to foot with a plainly appreciative appraisal. Just under her contained facade she was a turbulent woman, the fact there in her shining, black eyes.

"Are all the President's agents as handsome as you, Fargo?" Celia Downing smiled.

"Wouldn't know. Never met any of the others," he said. "Are there any other women as beautiful as you working for the general?" he slid at her and saw the pleased smile that touched the corners of her wide mouth, perhaps a fraction wider than Isabella's. He turned as a figure came through the doorway, short, clothed in a quasimilitary jacket with riding jodhpurs, eyes sharp and bright, black hair slicked back, and a fleshy face that fairly shouted self-indulgence with puffy cheeks and a thick lower lip. He was, Fargo thought, almost a caricature of a man with a bantam rooster walk.

Celia Downing pushed the note at Vargas. "Read this, Rolando," she said. The man took it from her and read it quickly as his brows lifted. He glanced up at Fargo with a sudden respect in his sharp, bright eyes.

"The President Buchanan sent you here?" he said, and Fargo nodded.

"Well, then you are most welcome, *Señor* Fargo," Vargas said with his faint Hispanic accent. "I presume he had a reason for sending you to see us."

"He did," Fargo said as Vargas handed him the letter of introduction back. Vargas cast a glance out one of the tall, arched windows.

"It will be time for dinner within the hour. Please be our guest. We do not often have a visitor of such importance. We can talk over some good wine. It is always more pleasant that way," the small man said.

"Can't disagree with that," Fargo said.

"Celia will show you where to clean up. I must finish with my men, and I'll see you at dinner," Vargas said and hurried out of the house.

"I'll get my travel bag," Fargo said, then went out to the Ovaro and returned to find Celia Downing waiting for him. She showed him to a spacious bathroom, appointed with fine, thick towels, and left him to wash and change into a clean shirt. Dinner would be a cat-and-mouse game, he realized, and he didn't dare underestimate Rolando Vargas's shrewdness. A portly, elderly servant waited as Fargo returned to the big study and led him to a handsome dining room with a long table set for three. Celia Downing appeared, and she had changed into a white gown, simple in lines with a deep V neck that showed the contours of her ample breasts.

Rolando Vargas appeared moments after, and Fargo saw that he had changed into a fancy, gold-braided military jacket of deep green with gold epaulettes. "You approve, my friend?" Vargas asked, noting Fargo's appraising glance. "I designed it myself."

"Very impressive," Fargo said, and Celia took the chair across from him at the table. The portly servant set a bottle of tequila in front of Vargas who quickly poured himself a drink and offered the bottle to Fargo.

"Later. I'll start with wine first," Fargo said and saw Celia's eyes flick to him as Vargas downed the shot glass of tequila and poured himself another.

"My lovely Celia and I have an arrangement. I do not touch a drop all day while I work hard, but I can have all I want after the sun goes down," Vargas said. Fargo glanced at Celia Downing who allowed a cool smile. "Now, *Señor* Fargo, why has President Buchanan sent you all the way down here to see me?" Vargas asked.

"Word is that you are training an army to invade Mexico," Fargo said.

"That's strange because my information tells me that not even Juarez is aware of this," Vargas said.

"That only shows how much better our channels are than his," Fargo said.

"I can believe that." Vargas nodded. "Juarez is a complacent fool."

Fargo turned to Celia as she cut in and Vargas took a third tequila. "I cannot believe that you were sent down here just to confirm that information. Surely President Buchanan has something more in mind," she said.

"He might have," Fargo said and let a note of slyness creep into his smile. "He'd like a few things answered."

"What kind of answers, my friend?" Vargas said, his speech quickly becoming slurred.

"The President would like to know if you really

have a plan to do this or is it just a wild adventure," Fargo said.

"Of course there is a plan, a very carefully thought-out plan," Vargas said, knocking over his glass and refilling it at once. "Once we take control of the Pinacate region, there will be thousands of men coming to join us. It will be the first spark of the revolution, the beginning of the fire," he said, growing excited over the thought and tossing off another tequila.

"Juarez has an army regiment in the Pinacate region. You'd have to destroy them first," Fargo said.

"We will, my friend, we will," Vargas slurred.

"With a hundred men? That's all I saw training," Fargo pressed.

"You have an expression, appearances are deceiving," Vargas said and gave an unsteady laugh. "Remember that, Fargo. There are many roads to victory."

Celia Downing interrupted, her voice firm. "This is not the time to discuss those matters, Rolando," she said. Vargas nodded and slumped back in his chair, his eyes closing. Fargo met Celia's steady stare.

"He listens to you," Fargo commented.

She offered a slightly smug smile. "He is smart enough to know he needs me in many ways," she said. "And I am smart enough to want to know what other things the President has asked you to find out."

Fargo smiled back and decided to toss out the next question just to see how she'd answer. "He'd like to know who is financing the general? Who's giving him the money to do this?" Fargo asked.

"I am," Celia Downing said, and Fargo smiled, but inwardly this time. She hadn't lied, but out of confidence or cleverness, honesty or arrogance, he asked himself. Perhaps it didn't much matter, he mused silently. "What else does he want to know?"

"If the general should overthrow Benito Juarez, is he capable of ruling Mexico?" Fargo asked, pulling the question out of midair as he cast a glance at Vargas who had passed out at the table.

"The evening makes you have some doubts." Celia smiled.

"Bull's-eye," Fargo admitted.

"Rolando is very capable in military affairs. I will be ruling the country on all other matters," the woman said. "Do you doubt my abilities, also, Fargo?"

"No, I sure don't," Fargo said.

"That's nice to hear," she said with a smile of private amusement.

"But I can't say I can send back a favorable report on the general's military capabilities. I haven't seen enough for that."

"And I can't show you more. I haven't heard enough from you for that," the woman said.

"You know how to bargain," Fargo said and laughed.

She shrugged at the compliment. "Why don't you spend the night, and we can talk more about this tomorrow," she suggested.

"Can't tonight," Fargo said. "I have to meet a courier who might just bring me some new instructions. But I'll come back tomorrow."

"Good enough, Fargo," she said, and when he gathered his things, she linked her arm in his as he walked outside. He glanced back to see two men carefully lifting Vargas and start to carry him away. "This is their job. I've hired them to do that. But do not underestimate Rolando. He will be fit and ready to train the men again tomorrow."

"And what will you be fit and ready for tomorrow?" Fargo questioned.

"To resume our conversation more deeply," the woman said.

"Sounds good to me," Fargo said. She took her arm from him as he climbed onto the Ovaro, and he saw her shining black eyes peering thoughtfully at him.

"You know, I think we might work very well together, Fargo," she said. "We can explore that, also, tomorrow."

"Why not?" Fargo said and rode from the compound, a sentry at an iron gate opening it for him. It had gone well, a good beginning. But he needed more time to examine the place more closely, more time to get Vargas and Celia to reveal more. As he rode north through the night, his thoughts went to Isabella. Why did she think her mother was Vargas's prisoner, he wondered. Did she think he wouldn't find out differently? The thought hung for a moment before he rejected it. She had asked him, if he got the chance, to tell her mother help was on the way. She really believed Celia Downing was being held prisoner, forced to help Vargas.

The next question asked itself. Why was she so wrong? What had happened to make belief and fact so far apart? The riddle rode with him, unanswered, but as he neared the ranch he had decided one thing; he'd not tell Isabella what he had found, not until after another visit to Celia Downing and Vargas and he pushed further speculation from his mind. Dawn was only a few hours away when he reached the ranch. He stabled the Ovaro and silently made his way to the guest room where the big bed was very welcoming. It was midmorning when he woke, and he had just washed and was only half dressed when Isabella burst into the room. "I went to the stable and saw the Ovaro," she said, clinging to him. "Why didn't you wake me?"

"I needed some hard sleep," he said.

Her hands pressed over his body, as if trying to make certain she wasn't dreaming. "You did it. You got in and out again," she breathed.

"I'm good at that," he said blandly and saw the color rise in her cheeks after a moment.

"Yes, but that's not what I meant," she said.

"I showed a letter from Buchanan. Vargas was very glad to see me. I'm going back again today," Fargo said. Isabella's face darkened with apprehension at once. "We'll be engaged in a kind of game. I want to keep him thinking I can help him, and he won't want to give out too much until he's sure I will. But I want the time for a better look around."

"Did you see my mother?" Isabella asked.

"No," he lied. "But I'm pretty sure where she is in the main house. I'll take a better look today." Isabella stepped aside to let him finish dressing and walked at his side to the stable. After he saddled the horse, she clung to him, lips full of warm sweetness, her breasts flattening against his chest as she held tightly to him. He looked down at her and again marveled at how much alike mother and daughter looked.

"I'm still afraid. Something could go wrong," Isabella said.

"Nothing will go wrong. I'm going on a fishing expedition with myself as the bait."

"Fishing for a slimy little fish," Isabella sniffed. "Will you be back again tomorrow?"

"Can't say," he answered. "Same as last time. Don't get upset too soon." She nodded and kissed him again before he climbed onto the pinto.

"Find a way to save my mother," she called after him as he rode from the ranch, and he heard the complete sincerity in her voice. He waved back, not at all certain he could do that, but determined to try to find out why Isabella remained so convinced her mother was a prisoner. He even wondered if he'd missed some subtleties during his last visit to Vargas. Perhaps Celia Downing wasn't as willing a partner as she had seemed. If not, she had sure put on a damn good act, he murmured and put the Ovaro into a fast canter.

7

It was early afternoon when Fargo reached Vargas's compound. The three men rode out to meet him again, but this time escorted him in without questions. Inside the compound Celia came forward beside Rolando Vargas; she wore a white blouse and black skirt. Fargo uttered a sound inside himself, once again made of awe as he took in the remarkable resemblance to Isabella. The real difference was not in the slightly fuller, bustier edition that was Celia, but in the shining, hard blackness of her eyes. Vargas, Fargo noted, seemed none the worse for his evening of hard drink, the man's self-indulgent, puffy-cheeked face showing none of the little red veins of the heavy drinker.

"We've been waiting for you, Fargo," Celia said with a smile that flashed a hint of a personal greeting.

"Did your courier arrive? Do you have new instructions," Vargas eagerly asked.

"Let's say some things were made more clear," Fargo said. "We can discuss those later."

"Of course. You'll have dinner with us again," Celia put in. "Meanwhile, Rolando will give you a full tour of the compound."

Fargo swung to the ground, and one of Vargas's men tethered the Ovaro outside the main house. The man who they referred to as General throughout the tour took Fargo to every section where his soldiers trained under individual instructors. With pompous pride, Vargas pointed out the way his men flung themselves into their training. "They are with me for more than money, Fargo. Their hearts are with me. Tell your President that," Vargas proclaimed. He led Fargo around the corrals and the collection of horses inside them, all good enough specimens, Fargo noted. Fargo asked about the big food-storage warehouse, and Vargas was quick to tell him how well-stocked it was.

"All for these hundred men?" Fargo remarked, sweeping over the soldiers at their maneuvers.

"I didn't say that, my friend," Vargas answered and looked pleased with himself.

"I know you must have many more men," Fargo said. "But I cannot tell the President that unless I've seen them."

Vargas smiled smugly again. "You can, when the time comes," he said.

"When will that be?" Fargo asked.

"When you have given us something besides questions," Vargas said.

"Sounds like Celia," Fargo commented.

"I listen to Celia in all negotiations. She is very smart woman," Vargas said, and Fargo's eyes went to a long line of Texas cotton-bed wagons outfitted with canvas tops, distinctly different from the Owensboro rigs along the food warehouse.

"How do you figure to use those?" Fargo asked.

Vargas returned a Cheshire cat smile. "To carry things. Wagons carry things," he said and strode away to show Fargo a large box of new carbines.

"Very nice," Fargo remarked. "It seems to me that you've everything under control. There's not much you seem to need."

Vargas's puffy-cheeked face puffed out further as

it filled with alarm. "Oh, no, Fargo, there is much that we can use. Juarez will throw his entire army at us in time," Vargas said. "We had a terrible setback only a few days ago. A major ammunition supply train exploded. Some idiot did something wrong and wiped out everything, including himself. There is some small justice in that. We can use many more arms and ammunition, gunpowder and dynamite. We could even use cannon. Juarez will have cannon."

Fargo let his lips purse. "You keep talking about Juarez. He's a long way down the road. You have to get past the Mexican garrison. I still haven't seen any sign you have the men or the equipment to do even that."

Vargas started to snap an answer and caught himself. "Celia will talk about that with you," he said, and Fargo smiled as he followed along. Vargas introduced him to some of his officers supervising marksmanship practice. They all wore a deep green version of Vargas's quasimilitary uniform with less gold braid than on his, but it did little to hide their very unmilitary roughness. They were men with the jaded eyes of mercenaries. Vargas was deluding himself if he thought these men followed him with their hearts. These men followed money, not ideals or ambitions. Yet as he walked on, he saw that some of the others, the infantrymen in training, were of a different stripe. Mostly Mexican, they trained with a fervor that came closer to what Vargas claimed he had in his troops.

They were a mixed bag, Fargo concluded, and he had seen armies led by mercenaries that were very effective. But there was nonetheless a ragtag air to the entire place that hardly inspired much confidence. Vargas would need something more to go up against a garrison of Mexican soldiers, and Fargo's eyes went to the long shed he'd noted the day before. Three sentries were again on guard outside it, apparently a permanent guard. The long shed held something Vargas kept guarded, and Fargo's lips thinned. He wanted a look inside that shed. He'd have to find a way, he promised himself. Questioning Vargas would bring the same kind of answer he got when asking about the canvas-topped wagons. He'd find out on his own, he murmured inwardly, and the day soon came to an end with Vargas still puffed with pride over what he'd shown.

He led the way back to the main house where Celia had changed to a deep blue version of the gown she'd worn the night before, the same low-cut V neckline showing the soft, curving edges of her breasts. Vargas reappeared in what was apparently his full-dress uniform attire, a white jacket with double rows of brass buttons and gold epaulettes. A servant placed a new bottle of tequila in front of him, and Vargas insisted Fargo join him and Celia in a toast. "To President Buchanan," he offered and downed his drink. "Will he send us help, Fargo? Will you tell him what you've seen?"

"I will," Fargo said.

"That's not enough," Celia put in with a smile. "Will you tell him we deserve help?"

"I just might," Fargo said carefully, and Rolando Vargas burst into a shout of joy, then followed it by downing two tequilas. Fargo felt Celia's eyes on him, probing, evaluating, plainly not taken by his answer. But she didn't challenge him on it, and the meal was served, antelope rabbit stew on a bed of rice.

"When can he send us help?" Vargas asked.

"Pretty quickly. Of course, that won't be my decision. I only can send in my report," Fargo said.

"To your report, my friend," Vargas said, rose, almost fell, and toppled back in his chair. But he kept a firm hold on the tequila and downed it in one gulp, slumping back. "This is wonderful, a great day," he slurred, eyes half closed, yet he managed to pour himself another drink.

Fargo turned to find Celia's eyes on him, a faint smile toying with the edges of her lips. "I pay more attention to words than Rolando does. He hears what he wants to hear," she said. Fargo glanced at Vargas. His head was back and his eyes were closed. He was already in a drunken stupor. "You have contempt for him, don't you?" Celia's voice asked. Fargo shrugged an answer. "You underestimate him. He is a brilliant, self-made field commander. He will defeat the garrison at Pinacate," Celia said.

"Not with a hundred men," Fargo put in.

She ignored his words. "But that will be only a first step. Your help from then on could be crucial. But then it really doesn't hang on your report, does it?" she said.

"How do you mean?"

"You have to help us," Celia said.

"Why?" Fargo questioned.

"Once Juarez finds out that an army has been raised and trained on American soil to overthrow him, he'll consider that a hostile act. He'll be forced to declare war on you. Your only choice is to help us crush him quickly." She finished with an almost triumphant smile.

"Maybe," Fargo agreed. "But maybe if we just stand back, it'll go another way." Celia questioned with her shining black eyes. "Juarez might just crush you and be grateful that we hung back."

"No. Once we crush the garrison at the Pinacate, there'll be thousands flocking to our side. The people do not like Juarez. There's talk that they'd be willing to accept the French puppet, Maximilian. They will come to us. The people respond to victory."

Fargo said nothing for a long moment. Giving it her own twist, her words had echoed what Buchanan had said about what Juarez might be forced to do. But Buchanan's solution had been a different one. Put an end to Vargas. To have a chance at that, he still needed more information. He had to draw her out more, put a dent in her contained composure. "I'm still bothered some," he said.

"About what?"

"You, mostly. I don't have a whole picture of you, Celia," he said. "I met Isabella." He paused, let the statement hang in front of her, and saw her brows lift. "She told me you were being held prisoner by Rolando. She really believes that," Fargo said.

Celia Downing let a moment pass before she smiled, a wry, almost sad smile. "Isabella is still a child, her head filled with idealistic notions and romantic fantasies. She could not accept the fact that I would go off with Rolando."

"Why not?"

"First, she has always disliked Rolando and, more important, he does not fit her idea of a lover, someone handsome and dashing."

Fargo cast a glance at the half-snoring Vargas. "He doesn't much fit mine, either," Fargo commented. "I agree with Isabella on that. Why did you, a woman with your looks, go off with him?"

"That's a kind of backhanded compliment, isn't it?" Celia remarked.

"Guess so."

"I didn't go off with Rolando because he was a great lover. He's pretty much a zero in that department," Celia said, and Fargo watched her black eyes narrow as she thought aloud. "I went with him because I've always wanted to be a woman of power. The idea has always fascinated me. When Rolando wins over Mexico, he will be *el Presidente*, and I will be his wife. As I'm sure you've already realized, I will be the real power. Rolando will strut and swagger, but he'll know I'm the power, his power as well as mine. He knows that now."

"I'd say he does," Fargo agreed and studied Celia Downing. She had been honest, laying it all out with no sugar coating. "And that's what you want. That'll be enough for you, that feeling of power?" Fargo asked.

"It's what I want. I didn't say it would be enough," Celia Downing said and clapped her hands sharply. The two men came into the room and again carefully carried Vargas away. Celia waited till they were gone before turning back to Fargo. "I'd like someone such as you with me, Fargo," she said. "Someone I could count on, in bed and out of bed. Maybe it was meant to be that you come here, that we meet each other."

"Hell, you're sounding like Isabella now," Fargo remarked. "Don't tell me you're a romantic, too, down deep inside yourself."

"No, I leave all that to Isabella. I'm a believer in reality, and coincidence is part of reality. I'm here for my reasons. You're here for yours. We're both here at the right place at the right time. That's coincidence. I say make the most of it."

"How?"

"You get Buchanan to help us, I promise you a powerful position in the new Mexico, one that'll make you a wealthy man," Celia said.

"I don't hold much store in future promises. Too many things can happen," Fargo said.

"How about something more immediate, then?"

Celia said. "A sample of what you'll have besides power and money."

"Why not?" he said, and Celia turned and beckoned leading the way down the wide corridor into a room where she lighted a lamp on low, and he saw a wide, large bed and a solid oak dresser with the top covered with bottles of lotion and powder and combs.

"My room," Celia said, and her hand went to the neckline of the gown, pulled something, and the gown fell open. She wriggled her shoulders, and it dropped to the floor. She stood before him, a tiny smile on her lips as she watched his eyes move across the full beauty of her. The pale olive skin was a shade darker than Isabella's, but only a shade, the breasts fuller, altogether larger, her body curvier, hips rounder, legs fleshier, thighs heavier, but a body charged with sensuousness. The jet black V was thick and very bushy, thrusting forward, an invitation of itself. He undid his gun belt and let it slide to the floor, then quickly shed clothes. Celia Downing lay back on the bed, across it sideways, as he came toward her, and this time it was her eyes that glowed with appreciation.

Her mouth opened, welcoming his, and Celia Downing's tongue thrust deep instantly, an eager messenger, a promise and a command, darting back and forth, and her mouth opened wider for him, enveloping, consuming. Her hands came alongside his face and held there as she drew back for breath. "Jesus, it's been so long, so long. And now suddenly you, too much, too much." She pulled his face from hers, pushed it down into her breasts, pressed his mouth against one full cup and cried out as his mouth closed over the dusty rose tip. He caressed with his tongue, circled, sucked, and Celia emitted a long, low moan and with one hand pressed her breast upward, pushing more of herself into his mouth.

She pulled her hand away, let it slide down his body, and found his erect, throbbing warmth and closed her fingers around him. "Oh, goddamn, goddamn," Celia flung out, and she was pulling at him, stroking, caressing, infusing herself with the erotic pleasures of the tactile senses. He kept his lips on one breast as his hand slid down, smoothed itself along the curves of her, over the rounded hump of her belly as she continued to pull at him and make gasping little sounds. He pushed through the dense whorls of her triangle, and her hips moved, then positioned themselves for him as she guided him to her. He felt the flowing lubricity of her at once as his pulsating organ touched against the soft flesh of her inner thighs, and Celia's voice rose and became a screamed command: "Come in . . . come in, oh, Jesus, take me, take me."

He slid forward and her fleshy thighs came against him instantly. No sweet surging offering for Celia. Her torso came up and she bucked under him, slammed herself upward and forward, guttural cries that matched each wild heaving. He quickly matched her rough intenseness, ramming into her, and she cried out with pleasure, half screams that held the edge of wild laughter in them. His face bent forward against the tossing breasts as Celia Downing screamed and twisted and bucked and her guttural cries became wilder, beyond her control, and she was screaming and laughing and crying then laughing again. "Yes, yes, yes, yes . . . aaagh . . . aaagh, oh, Jesus, yes," she flung out, and she was flowing hotly against him. Suddenly he saw her arms straighten out stiffly, and her torso rose, her fists beating wildly against the bedsheet, and he felt her thighs pressing hard into his sides.

Her fists continued to pound against the bed as he felt her inner spasms flow around him. When a long, almost anguished sigh came from deep inside her, she finally fell back onto the bed, keeping him inside her as her breathing came in short, harsh gasps. He lay with her, and a long tremor came, coursed through her, and her thighs fell away from him as her eyes opened, shining blackness peering up at him. "God, it's been so long. You have to stay here. This is what it'll be: me, money, position."

"What happens to Rolando?" Fargo asked.

"I know he'll drink even more after we win. A doctor told me he can't take much more of that. Then there'll be just the two of us."

"Madame Presidente and me," Fargo said.

"Sounds wonderful to me," Celia Downing said, and her hand reached down as he slid from her to cup him, holding him gently.

"Just curious, but what happens to Isabella. You expect she'll follow down here after you?" Fargo asked.

"Never. She can have the ranch and her romantic fantasies," Celia said and cast a sidelong glance at him. "Though she might approve of you physically. Emotionally, she'd see you as just another fortune hunter."

"Probably," Fargo said blandly.

"She's a perfect example of being burdened by ideals," Celia said.

"Not something that's ever burdened you," Fargo commented.

"That's right." Celia sniffed. "Too bad for her because she is quite beautiful, but I suppose you noticed that."

"I did," Fargo said. "And now I know where she gets her looks."

Celia sat up, and her arms went around him as she pressed herself to him. "Compliments. Oh, I'm going to like having you around, Fargo," she murmured. He stifled the wry sound that rose up inside him. Celia had passed more than her physical beauty on to Isabella. She had made Isabella what she was and was plainly completely unaware of it. Isabella had become a romantic idealist because she couldn't stand her mother's cynical, absolute selfishness. It had been a flight for her. She had fled to another world where it was a better place, where she could believe in all good things turning out in the best way. He suddenly felt terribly sorry for Isabella. Reality would be a thing of terrible harshness. "What are you going to report to your President, Fargo?" Celia's voice asked, bringing him back to his own reality. "Tell him we need money, guns, and ammunition, mostly money. We can buy our arms."

"I want to know how many men you have," Fargo said. "I can't ask for his help without that."

"Tell him we have enough for the first step, crushing the garrison in Pinacate," Celia said, and Fargo smiled. She remained cagey, unwilling to yield more than she had.

"Where are they?" he asked.

"You will find out when the time comes," Celia said.

"I could think you don't trust me," Fargo said and let himself sound hurt.

"I'll trust you more after you show me your report," she said. "I trust you in bed. That will have to do for now." Her hand reached out, took hold of his, and began to stroke gently. "This will have to do for now. I'll show you how much I want you.

This will be our trust," she said and brought her face down to his groin, pressing, sliding, nibbling, then her mouth opening. Celia made good on her word as she sent the night into a time of total sensuousness, her eager wanting riding over all else, consuming everything in its devouring hunger. Once again her screams echoed through the room, her torso slamming hard against his and her full-cupped breasts pushing into his mouth. And again there was no sweet surging to Celia, only the total, gratifying fire of flesh to flesh until finally she lay beside him, breathing heavily, and he let her slowly gather herself.

He smiled to himself. She had wanted him, totally and absolutely. There had been no question. But she had also used her body to try and make him forget his questioning. He'd let her think she had succeeded, and he sat up as she swung to the edge of the bed. "You can spend the night soon, but not yet, not until Rolando asks you. He can have fits of childish jealousy," Celia said.

"Understandable," Fargo said as he pulled on clothes.

"He will wake in another hour and, half drunk, he'll still call for me. I must be there. Of course, he'll fall asleep again," Celia said and, the gown around her, she brought her lips to Fargo again. "Go back, write your report," she said.

"You have a one-track mind, Celia." Fargo smiled.

"That's how I get what I want," she tossed back and walked to the door with him, closing it silently as he slipped out into the dark night. He waited and let his eyes move slowly across the darkened buildings of the compound to halt at the long, low structure where the three guards were stationed, one on each side of the building and one outside the front door. Fargo's eyes narrowed. He desperately wanted to see what was inside the building, and this might well be his only chance. He had to take it, he muttered, then untethered the Ovaro and led the horse slowly along one side of the compound wall. When he reached the food warehouse, he brought the horse behind the building, dropped the reins to the ground, and the pinto came to a halt. Fargo crept forward along the warehouse until he reached the back, from which he could approach the long, low building from the rear. He moved forward and darted sideways until he was directly behind the structure and then went forward in a low, loping crouch. He came up against the rear of the building and halted for a moment, listening. There was no sound from the guards, and he moved to the corner, then peered around it to see the guard against the side of the building, his eyes half closed as he leaned backward.

Fargo's hand started to reach for the throwing knife, but pulled back. He wanted silence, but not killing, so he drew the Colt instead, and turned the revolver in his hand to grip the barrel. Gathering himself, he whipped around the corner and raced toward the guard. The man pulled his eyes around, started to straighten and bring his rifle around, but Fargo was at him, chopping the butt of the Colt downward. The sentry, his mouth still open, crumpled to the ground, and Fargo caught the rifle before it fell from his hand. He propped the sentry up in a sitting position against the wall and laid his rifle a dozen feet from him. Moving forward on steps silent as a lynx, Fargo halted to peer carefully around the corner of the structure.

The second guard stood directly in front of the door of the shed, holding his rifle casually, the stock resting on the ground. He wasn't half asleep as was the first one, but he was only half the distance away. Again, Fargo whipped around the corner of the shed and raced forward, but this time the butt of the Colt was in his hand. The guard whirled and started to raise his rifle to find the barrel of the Colt in front of his face. He froze, swallowed hard, and blinked. "Turn around, slowly," Fargo whispered, keeping the revolver pointed at the man's face. The guard turned, a man plainly disinclined to heroics, and Fargo brought the gun down on the back of his head. Fargo held him as he collapsed, closing both arms around him and the rifle. He lowered both to the ground and propped the man up against the front of the shed, to one side of the door.

He and the other guard would be unconscious long enough for him to see what was stored in the shed, Fargo was certain as he decided to leave the third sentry untouched on the other side of the building. He stepped to the door and was grateful to see no padlock on it. Vargas trusted his guards, another example of his confident cockiness. Fargo quietly turned the doorknob, eased the door open, and closed it behind him to stand unmoving inside the long shed, letting his eyes adjust to the blackness. Two tall windows admitted enough moonlight to let him begin to discern a double row of canvas-covered objects. He moved to the nearest one, pulled the canvas from it, and stared down at a small cannon mounted on a moveable carriage. A longer look showed him it was not a cannon but the lighter carronade that had been developed for use aboard naval ships.

Taking the canvas from the next six objects, he found they all were carronades, each with three tin canisters filled with small lead musket balls. These had been designed as antipersonnel weapons and when fired by the carronades, gave the effect of a gigantic shotgun blast. He moved down the rows, peering under each of the other canvas covers and found a carronade and canisters under each. When he finished, he replaced the six covers he had removed entirely and leaned back against a wall, his lips pursed in thought. Rolando Vargas was indeed not to be underestimated. He didn't need to outnumber the Mexican garrison in the Pinacate. He had prepared a surprise for them that would sure as hell win the battle for him. The canvas-topped Texas cotton-bed wagons were also suddenly explained. Each would carry one of the carronades. At the right time the canvas tops would be pulled back and the guns fired.

The Mexicans would be decimated and Vargas's army would do the rest. The carronades wouldn't be Vargas's only surprise, Fargo was certain now. The self-styled general had a sizable force somewhere. Suddenly, Vargas was not just a pompous, almost laughable little rooster, but a real danger. It was no longer a matter of keeping him from creating an awkward situation with the Mexicans. He was going to win his first strike against the garrison in the Pinacate, and that would sure as hell create a crisis with the Juarez government. Vargas had to be stopped. That mission had suddenly taken on a new importance.

Fargo's lips pulled back in a grimace. He knew what had to be done, but he wasn't at all sure how to do it. Perhaps it was time to contact Major Grady at Gila Bend. But Buchanan had warned him that the major hadn't more than two hundred men. Were two hundred men enough to put an end to Vargas? Or would he be calling two hundred men to their deaths? If attacked, Vargas would use his carronades. Surprise would be vital. But the outcome would really depend on how many men Vargas had hidden away. After finding the carronades, Fargo knew he could no longer discount the pompous little man. He straightened, pushed aside further thoughts, and moved toward the door. He'd go back to the ranch and figure out a way to find out what he had to know. Perhaps the way would be through Celia, he pondered as he reached the door, opened it just enough to slip through, and stepped outside.

He came to a dead halt. Celia waited there, three men with rifles behind her, the guns all trained on him. "I'm really very disappointed, Fargo," she said. "Terribly."

8

"I wasn't getting answers," Fargo said. "Thought I'd see for myself."

Celia's black eyes peered hard at him. She wore a tan robe that covered her with proper modesty. "Get his gun," she said to one of the men without taking her eyes off Fargo. "He wears a knife in a calf-holster around his leg, too," she added. While the other two kept their rifles trained on him, the man came forward and followed orders. Fargo eyed the other two guns. They were too steady and too close. Heroics would only bring bullets, he decided. Celia continued to let her black, shining eyes bore into him. "I don't like this at all, none of it, Fargo," she said. "I'm not sure what it means."

"I told you, I was curious," Fargo said.

"Curious for whom?" Celia said.

"For President Buchanan," Fargo told her.

"I don't know that I believe that any longer," Celia said.

"I showed you his letter," Fargo said.

"It could be a fake," she said.

"You saw the seal on it."

"I saw a seal. I don't know if it was the real thing," Celia returned sharply. "I told you I'd tell you more when the time came. Why didn't you leave it at that?"

"That didn't satisfy me."

"I'm going to have to think about you, Fargo," she said. "I'm very bothered by this."

"You're making too much out of it," Fargo said almost chidingly.

Celia continued to regard him thoughtfully. "Maybe, but then maybe I'm not making enough out of it," she said and stretched a hand out to the man with the Colt and the throwing knife. "I'll take those," she said. "Put him in the guardhouse—three guards outside and keep the door locked."

"How'd you know I was in here?" he asked as the men prodded him with their rifles.

"After I looked in on Rolando, I went outside for a little walk. I often do. I saw the sentries here sitting down against the shed. I went over to give them a piece of my mind. I knew it was you, at once," she said and turned on her heel and strode away.

Fargo was led to a square structure with two barred windows where the door was opened and he was flung inside. The stub of a candle burned in one corner, and he saw an interior with a narrow cot and a toilet hole in the far corner. A pitcher of water rested near the cot. "You sure it's not too fancy," Fargo commented.

"Nobody stays here long, mister," one of the men growled as the door was pulled shut, and Fargo heard the outside bolt slide into place. He sat down on the cot and swore softly at himself. The unexpected had happened, and he was paying the price. His best hope now, strangely enough, was Celia. Her cynical, self-centered ambition wouldn't permit her to write him off yet. So long as she was still uncertain about him, she'd do nothing she couldn't take back. He had to keep her uncertain. It'd be a tightrope, but it was all he had. He stretched out on the cot and let himself doze in fitful spurts. The morning dawned, sun finding its way through the two barred windows, and he woke, blew out the candle, and dozed again. When he woke again, the sun had passed midmorning. He washed with the contents of the pitcher, tepid water, and was sitting up when he heard the door open.

A woman wearing a shawl over her head brought him a tray of food, two guards watching from the doorway until she withdrew. He ate the hard roll and drank the thin coffee, and when she returned, she had another, full clay pitcher of water to replace the old one. The door was locked again, and Fargo found that by moving the cot and standing on it, he could peer out one of the high windows. The compound stretched out before him, the wall around the three sides, and he could see part of the main house. He could also glimpse some of the squads in training and hear the others.

He tested the bars and swore softly. They were all solidly embedded in the window. Suddenly, as he watched, he saw Celia come into view, walking from the house toward him. He dropped from the cot, pushed it back into place, and was waiting as the outside bolt was opened and she came into the jail. "Stay outside," she told the guards and pulled the door closed behind her. "I've been wrestling with this all day, Fargo," she said, drawing a deep breath that pushed her full breasts into the white shirt she wore.

"You tell Rolando I'm here?" he asked, and her brows lifted.

"Did you think I wouldn't?" she asked.

"I wondered," Fargo said.

"He'd see the guards and ask," Celia said. "I had to tell him."

Fargo smiled. "Otherwise you wouldn't have."

Celia's black eyes sparked dark fire at him.

"You're in no position to be flippant with me, Fargo."

"Not being flippant, just telling the truth. He hasn't come around. You saw to that, too," Fargo said. "You're afraid I might tell him about everything that happened last night."

"I'd say you were lying. He'd believe me," she said.

Fargo smiled at her again. "You're not sure of that, honey, and you know it." Her eyes narrowed at him, and he laughed softly. "Bull's-eye," he said.

Celia's hand came up in a short arc, and he caught her wrist before the blow landed on his cheek, held it, and pressed his mouth on hers. She resisted, then he felt her lips soften. He let her wrist go after a moment and stepped back. "Damn you," she hissed.

"What'd you tell Rolando?" Fargo asked.

"I told him that maybe you were just being curious and we shouldn't be hasty," she said.

"Very good," Fargo said. "Especially as how that's the truth."

"He asked what if you were a spy, maybe someone Juarez hired. It's possible word has come to him," Celia said.

"You said what if I weren't. What if I was going to get Buchanan to help you," Fargo offered.

"That's right," she said. "Which is it, Fargo?"

"The President sent me. That's the truth of it. And last night you made me the kind of offer a man would be a fool to turn down," Fargo said, the answer absolutely honest.

Celia's eyes remained narrowed. "I can't see you as a fool," she said. "But then you just might be." He smiled back.

"It's Isabella's world that's made of fools and romantics," he said.

"I have to think more about this, Fargo," Celia said as she moved toward the door. He strode after her and came up against her.

"You'll come up with the right answer," he said.

"How do you know?"

"You can't stop thinking about last night," he said, his hands cupping her breasts as he pushed hard against her. She gave a tiny gasp before she moved away, black eyes fastened on him as she rested one hand on the doorknob.

"You're right, I can't," Celia said. "But you should know one thing. If I decide you're too much of a risk, I'll have you shot."

Fargo kept the confidence in his smile. "You won't decide that," he said, and she didn't answer as she left and closed the door behind her. His smile vanished. He wasn't at all sure what Celia would do. He was still walking the tightrope, and there was nothing else he could do. But it had gone well so far, he consoled himself and sat down on the cot. Darkness came when the woman in the shawl was admitted with a tray of supper, pieces of chicken bone with scraps of meat attached and a soup that seemed more water than anything else. He lay down on the cot after the woman came for the tray and let the cell stay in darkness except for the moonlight that found its way through the two windows.

He fell half asleep, woke, dozed again, and realized the waiting and wondering was fraying his nerves. He rose and started to pull the cot beneath the window so he could peer outside when he heard the sound at the door and quickly stretched out on the cot, hands behind his head. He stayed that way as the door opened and Celia entered. She snapped words at the guard, and Fargo heard the bolt slide closed. He swung from the cot. "Rolando passed out again?" he asked, and Celia nodded. "You've done your deciding?" he questioned.

"I have," she said and stepped to him, and he saw she wore the dark robe. She pulled the waist string, and the robe fell open, and he saw her nakedness underneath. A shrug of her shoulders and the robe fell away entirely, and she came to him, her rounded, sensual figure pale in the moonlight, her hair and triangle blacker than ever by contrast. "The walls are real thick," she said, her arms rising up and starting to pull at his belt. He let her, then shed clothes quickly, and she was atop him on the cot, rubbing her bushy nap up and down over him as he felt himself respond. "Yes, oh yes," Celia breathed as he rose, swelling at once to seek her. She drew her thighs up, then pressed them down against him and brought her moist entranceway to him. "Oh, God," she moaned as he found her, pushed upward, and her full rear rose up, came down again, rose and fell, and her gasped sounds buried themselves into his chest.

She rolled as he turned to bring himself atop her, and her belly came up to press against his groin as she pushed to match his every slow thrust. She pulled his head down to her breasts, and he took first one, then the other, as he moved with her. Celia's mouth pressed into the side of his neck, tiny muffled cries coming from her as her body twisted and leaped with him. "Yes, oh, God, more, more, oh more," he heard her gasp out, thrusting furiously with him, demanding every ounce of ecstasy her frenzied flesh could bring. He answered, swept forward by her demanding, devouring hunger. When she finally slammed her pubic mound against him with a last furious spasm, her mouth against his chest muffled the scream that tore through her as he continued to thrust inside her, not stopping as

117

she gasped and cried out and finally fell away, her curving form limp. "No more, oh, God, no more . . . oh, ooooh," Celia groaned and he fell upon her, completely expended.

Her breasts rose and fell against him as she gasped in deep draughts of air, and finally, normal breathing returned. She moved, and he slid from her as she pushed up to sit at the edge of the cot. "It was wonderful, everything I expected, everything I wanted," Celia said as she rose, picked up the robe and slowly put it around her. Fargo swung from the cot, his eyes on her as he pulled on trousers and boots. He straightened and donned his shirt as Celia looked on.

"Do I leave with you now?" he asked. "Or have you arranged for Rolando to let me go come morning?" Celia said nothing, but her little smile stayed wistfully sad, a strange quality in it, and he felt the furrow across his brow. She continued to remain silent, and her black eyes regarded him regretfully. The furrow on his brow turned into a frown, and as he searched her face, the realization was a sudden explosion inside him. "Goddamn. You're not letting me go, are you?" he hissed.

Celia offered an apologetic half shrug to go with the sad little smile. "I'm sorry, I just can't trust you anymore. It would have been so nice, but I can't take the chance. Orders have been given to have you shot at dawn," she said.

"What the hell was all that about just now?" Fargo snapped at her.

"Pleasure. My pleasure," Celia said wistfully. "It will be a long dry spell. It seemed such a terrible waste not to enjoy you once again."

"You bitch. You stinking, rotten bitch," Fargo rasped.

"Most men don't get to die on such a pleasant

note. The condemned man had a hearty screw," Celia said and turned for the door. Fargo's reaction was instant, made of fury more than thought. His fist shot out and caught her alongside the jaw. She went down. It was now or never, he swore at himself as he stepped over her and pounded on the door.

"Get in here," he shouted. "The madam's fainted. Get in here." He stepped to one side as he heard the bolt being slid open. One of the guards came in, saw Celia, and rushed to her. The second one followed, more cautiously, rifle in his hands as he gestured to Fargo.

"Get back," he said. Fargo started to obey and whipped his hands out, seized the rifle, and twisted it from the man's grip as his knee plunged into the guard's groin. The guard sank to the ground, clutching himself in pain, and Fargo saw the sentry kneeling beside Celia turn to him and start to bring his gun up. Fargo smashed the rifle stock into his face, and he toppled sideways and lay still. Pushing the door shut, Fargo stripped the shirt from the second guard, tore it into strips, and fashioned gags for both men and Celia. He used the rest of the shirt to bind their ankles, then their hands behind their backs. Taking one of the rifles, he stepped outside and pushed the bolt into place. He paused and let his eyes sweep the compound. Nothing moved, and he went into a long, loping crouch to make his way to the main house.

The door opened, and he hurried down the wide corridor to Celia's room and allowed a grim smile of satisfaction. He had guessed right, his Colt and throwing knife were atop her dresser. He put both weapons in their rightful places and ran from the house. The next stop was the stable where he quickly found the Ovaro, saddled the horse, and rode slowly across the compound. He moved through the gate, then turned the horse sharply and headed toward the sloping land behind the compound. He was almost at the start of the slope when he caught movement out of the corner of his eye at the side wall of the compound. Keeping his distance, he moved the Ovaro to his left where he could get a better view and reined to a halt as he saw the lone figure, clothed in black shirt and black jeans, tossing the grappling hook up at the top of the wall.

"Shit," he breathed as he saw the grappling hook catch hold, and the figure began to pull itself up the side of the wall. He dug heels into the horse's sides, and the Ovaro went into an instant gallop. Fargo flew the short distance across the flat ground to the wall and reached it just as the figure neared the top of the wall. He closed one hand around the rope and yanked on it. The figure peered down in alarm, jet black hair falling over her face. "Get the hell down here," he hissed, and she let herself slide downward. He grabbed hold of her with one arm as she reached him and swung her onto the pinto. She peered at him with eyes round and wide. "Where's your horse?" he asked, and she pointed to a cluster of piñon oak halfway up the other side of the slope. He sent the Ovaro racing for it as he hissed at her. "Don't talk," he said as they galloped to the trees where she slid down, then emerged on the cinder gray mount.

She swung alongside him as he set a fast pace up the slope, but she reined to a sudden halt. "We can't go without my mother," she said.

"Yes, we can," he told her. "We can't get her out, not tonight. Take my word for it." She followed him as he rode on, her lips turned down unhappily, and he halted only when they were more than far enough from the compound. He peered at Isabella in exasperation. "I don't know whether to kiss you or turn you over my knee," he said.

"Try the first," she said, and he leaned over and tasted the sweetness of her lips. "You didn't come back. I knew something was wrong," she said. "I decided to come get you."

"And maybe get yourself killed," he said.

She shrugged. "I didn't plan on that happening," she said and gave a sudden smile. "The grappling hook worked perfectly. I'd have been over the top in another minute if you hadn't stopped me. All that training wasn't wasted."

"Not yet," he agreed.

"You want to tell me what happened? Were you riding out or escaping?" Isabella asked.

"Escaping," he said and chose phrases carefully. "I did some snooping, found out a few things, and Vargas didn't like it. He was going to have me shot come dawn."

"But you managed to get out before I got to you," Isabella said. "Did you see my mother?"

"Yes," Fargo said. "She's all right."

"Can we get her out of there?"

"We'll talk about that after I get some sleep," Fargo said. "There's a lot more than that we have to do and do fast." She frowned, but he didn't spell out anything more, and she fell silent until they reached the ranch.

"I'll stable the horses," she said. "You get some sleep. You look as though you need it."

"Best idea I've heard in a long time," he said and found his way to the guest room as Isabella led the Ovaro away. He shed his clothes and realized he hadn't really slept that much for two nights as exhaustion pulled at him. Sleep was quick and welcome and lasted till the morning sun was high when he woke, washed, and found his way to the kitchen. One of the women gave him coffee, and the corn cakes tasted better than any he'd ever had. He was finished when Isabella came in and leaned her head on his chest.

"You're back. That's what counts," she said, stepping away to search his face. "With trouble in your eyes," she said, sitting down with him.

"Vargas is more dangerous than anyone's thought," Fargo said. "We have to find out how much of an army he has and where they're hidden. I'm afraid what happened with me is going to make him advance his schedule. He'll want to move, have himself a victory, before I can get to anyone."

"How can we do that?" Isabella asked.

"I have to think that out yet," Fargo said unhappily.

"What about my mother? You said you saw her," Isabella asked, and Fargo met her wide, anxious eyes. The truth would destroy her, he knew, yet he couldn't avoid it forever. He'd bring her to it slowly, he decided, plant the seeds that might help cushion the harshness of truth when she had to face it.

"What if things aren't the way you think they are?" he slid at her.

"Meaning exactly what?" She frowned.

"What if your mother isn't being held prisoner?" he asked.

Isabella's eyes flashed. "Of course she is. What makes you say a thing like that?"

"It's just that I didn't see any guards around her," Fargo said carefully. "She seemed to move about freely."

"Just because you didn't see them doesn't mean they weren't there. Vargas is clever," Isabella said.

"I suppose so," Fargo agreed. "But he introduced me to your mother. I had a little time alone with her. She didn't say anything about being held prisoner."

"Of course not. You had come to see Vargas. She didn't know whether to trust you or not," Isabella countered.

"Guess not," Fargo said. "I just wondered if you'd thought about it. After all, she did go off with him."

"No, it's not possible," Isabella said, dismissing his remark, so he shrugged and pursued it no further. Truth was seldom a match for faith, especially self-generated faith. But he had planted a seed. It would stay, he knew, despite her dismissal.

"We'll talk more later," he said. "I'm going out riding alone, to look and to think."

"Take me. I won't say a word," Isabella promised.

"Distractions don't have to say anything," he told her, and she gave a quietly pleased little smile as she left.

He saddled the Ovaro and spent the rest of the day exploring the hard, dry basalt terrain, venturing into an arroyo where life suddenly appeared in the honeybees among the prickly-pear blossoms and clusters of silvery wild zinnias. Cactus wrens and Gila woodpeckers flew past, and he was surprised to see the scarlet feathers of a cardinal. When he finally returned to the ranch, the sky had become deep purple streaked with red as dusk swept over the land. But he had decided upon a plan, such as it was, and he talked to Isabella about it over a meal of rice and a mixture of antelope rabbit and chicken.

"Pick out six of my best people?" she echoed.

"Yes. I want a constant watch on the compound," Fargo said. "I want to know when Vargas moves that food he has stored away. It's got to be to feed his hidden army."

"All right, but why six to watch his place?" Isabella questioned.

"Only one will be directly watching his place," Fargo said. "But for one rider to come all the way back here to tell us Vargas is moving his wagons will take much too long. He might have disappeared before we can get back there. So we'll set up a relay system of six men. The one watching the compound will pass the word to the second one a mile back, the second to the third until the sixth one can race here with it. It'll save hours."

"And then?"

"When I get the word, I'll be off and racing to tail Vargas's wagons before they disappear," Fargo said.

"*We'll* be off and racing," Isabella corrected, and he didn't disagree. He'd no idea what he'd find, and she could possibly be of help. Besides, she wouldn't stay away. He smiled to himself. It was too much her mission. "I'll go pick out the six men and explain what they'll be doing," Isabella said. "Shall I send them right out tonight?"

"Yes." Fargo nodded. "I don't know how nervous I've made Vargas. Let's not mess up."

She hurried away, and Fargo rose from the table and went to the guest room where he stretched out on the bed, leaving the door open. When Isabella came in, she closed it behind her and sat on the edge of the bed. "It's done. They are on their way," she said. "I told them it wasn't likely Vargas would be moving the food wagons in broad daylight so they could rest after sunup."

"That's probably right," Fargo agreed.

"You can rest after sunup, too," she said as she pulled her blouse off. It was not an idle remark, he learned. Isabella came to him, made of guileless yearning, and he realized her lovemaking was an extension of her romantic self, a sweet eroticism, contradictory as that seemed. Form follows function, he knew, and perhaps the flesh follows the spirit. It was a lazy afterthought when the sun came up and Isabella slept against him, softly curved breasts pressed into his chest, her handsomeness with a little-girl quality to it asleep. She had been sweepingly satisfying and satisfied. "You are my special one," she whispered to him in between bouts of ecstasy and somehow evoked a tenderness inside him for her. That was a feeling Celia could never and would never evoke.

When he finally rose with Isabella, she returned to her room and joined him again later in the day as he scanned the distant land. "You can't hide an army under a few ridges or in a handful of arroyos or dry washes, even a small one. Where has he got them, dammit?" Fargo said, thinking aloud.

"Maybe he hasn't much of a force. Maybe he's trying to bluff his way," Isabella suggested.

"I wondered about that, but not anymore, not after finding the carronades," Fargo said. "He has his army someplace. The only question is how much of one." Fargo lapsed into silence, and he was still turning thoughts in his mind as the day drew to a close. He found himself sitting across from Isabella in the large living room. "If Vargas decides he has to make his move, everything he's prepared will fall into place. We won't have time to think about what we have to do. Everything I can know now is important. Do you know where the Mexican garrison is stationed in the Pinacate?"

"At Los Vidrios, I've been told. That's just across the border east of us," Isabella said.

"Which means Vargas will cross near the compound and immediately turn east on the relatively flat land along the border." Fargo frowned. He summoned a mental map for himself as he grimaced. "The cavalry troop at Gila Bend would need at least a day, maybe closer to two, to reach the border. And that's only after we communicate with Major Grady. I don't like the way it's shaping up."

"There's nothing you can do about time and distance, my love," Isabella said gently.

"Use them, work around them, find a way," Fargo bit out angrily. He continued thinking aloud with Isabella when he heard the sound of a horse galloping to a halt outside. Isabella ran to the door with him.

"It's Rojas, last of the relays," Isabella said as the rider leaped to the ground.

"The wagons are moving out of the compound," he said and Fargo was already running toward the Ovaro, motioning for Isabella to follow. She ran to the cinder gray horse and caught up to him as he raced the Ovaro south toward the compound.

"With the time we saved by the relays I figure they won't have more than a two-hour head start, and the wagons will be moving slowly," Fargo said. "We shouldn't have trouble catching them." But he kept the Ovaro at close to a gallop, and they passed the other relay riders as they raced through the early night. Finally, they reached the man watching the compound, and he rose to his feet as they halted.

"They go northeast. Vargas is with them," he said.

"Good work," Fargo said and turned the Ovaro up a long slope, his eyes surveying the ground. Mostly stone, a cover of loose pebbles let him see where the wagon tracks had rolled upward. He guessed they had ridden another hour when he came in sight of the dark bulky shapes that rolled single file through the hill passages. He slowed, hung back, and let the Ovaro go to a walk. "They keep moving north and upland," Fargo said, and Isabella frowned as she nodded. With surprise he saw the wagons being hauled farther up into the lava stone, winding paths forming slow circles as they continued upward. He saw Isabella's frown as she rode beside him. "Talk," he said. "Where are we? Where's he going?"

"We're in the old volcano formations," she said, and the frown stayed on her brow. Fargo echoed her frown as he watched the wagons circle, then cut along a narrow, basalt passage and come to a halt. "Of course," Isabella hissed, and her hand came out to close around his arm. "The *calderas*, inside the *calderas*," she said.

"What are the *calderas*?"

"Giant craters, made when the undersurface of the old volcanoes collapsed millions of years ago," Isabella said. "They are mostly very large depressions with sloping sides. Some are over a mile wide and eight hundred feet deep. These are not that big, but they're big enough to hold a lot of men."

Fargo dismounted, left the horses where they were, and moved forward on foot with Isabella. He halted and dropped out of sight behind a tall, jagged rock where they had a clear view of three large craters connected by the high passage where the wagons were stopped. He saw the figures climbing out of the craters as he watched, moving to the wagons, lining up on the edge of the passage, and he cursed softly as the figures kept emerging from the deep craters. The wagon drivers began to unload the sacks of food, tossing some down the slopes of the *calderas* as the men lined up. Fargo squinted through the moonlit night and made a fast estimate, counting figures in groups of tens. "Shit," he muttered. "I make four hundred men. Five with the hundred at the compound. With the carronades he figures to make it in his favor, even with the Mexican garrison at a thousand."

Isabella turned and stared at him. "Where did you hear the Mexican garrison is a thousand men?" she queried.

"I figured a major garrison would have that much strength," Fargo said.

"They've been undermanned for years. I have a cousin with the Mexican general staff. There aren't more than four hundred men at the Pinacate garrison," Isabella said, and Fargo felt a sinking feeling in the pit of his stomach.

"With the carronades Vargas will have a three-to-one advantage," he said, grimness settling over him as Isabella touched his arm and motioned to the wagons. He saw Vargas atop the driver's seat of the first wagon.

"The time has come," Vargas said to the assembled figures, speaking in English and then in Spanish. "You will have a good meal tonight in your *calderas*. Tomorrow night you will leave and march to the compound. You will reach it before dawn and take four hours sleep. Your horses will be ready for you, as will your guns. We will cross into Mexico and destroy the Pinacate garrison at dawn the next day. It will be the beginning of the new government of Mexico." He stepped down to a chorus of cheers, and Fargo backed away from their rocky vantage point.

"Let's go," he said. "I've heard enough." Isabella retrieved her cinder gray mount as he climbed onto the Ovaro and let him ride back to the ranch in silence. Only when they reached the ranch did she speak.

"Can we do anything?" she asked. "Or is it beyond reach?"

"It's damn close to that," Fargo said as they stabled the horses and she went to bed with him to lay close against him, offering her warm nakedness as comfort. There was a slim chance. Everything had to go right for it to succeed. He had turned it over in his mind on the ride back, and he wanted to sleep on it, let the inner mind decide for him.

"I will be with you, whatever you decide," Isabella murmured.

"Get some sleep," he told her and held her to him. Maybe she would play the key role before it was over. It might be only fitting, he mused as he closed his eyes.

9

He woke with the new day, his mind made up, mostly because the subconscious had brought him no other plan. Isabella's eyes questioned him over breakfast, and he wanted to sound hopeful for her, but knew he only sounded grim. "Vargas is using surprise as one of his weapons, an army to surprise the garrison at the Pinacate, an attack to add to that surprise, and his carronades as the final surprise," Fargo said. "Our only chance is to do some surprising ourselves."

"How?" Isabella frowned.

"First, take away the surprise he's counting on. I'm going to ride to the Mexicans and see the commander of the garrison. I'll lay it all out for him."

"Will he believe you?" Isabella asked.

Fargo's face screwed up in distaste. "I don't know. I've got to convince him. He's got to be ready for Vargas's attack. That's the first surprise we'll turn back on Vargas."

"I'll go with you. He can't disbelieve the two of us," Isabella offered.

"Maybe not, but you can't go with me. I'm counting on you for something more important. You're going to ride to Major Grady at Gila Bend and bring his company back with you," Fargo said and watched her eyes widen.

"I am?" she gasped.

"You use my name. The major knows I'm out here for Buchanan. You explain he's going to the rescue of the Mexican garrison, and you lead him across the border to Los Vidrios. I figure it'll be a two-day ride for you to get there and come back with the cavalry. Vargas will be fighting with the garrison by then, though I hope not doing as well as he expected. Grady's cavalry coming up at his rear will be our second surprise."

"What if it doesn't go right? What if you can't convince the commander at the garrison, and Vargas takes him by surprise? What if I don't arrive in time with Grady's cavalry?" Isabella asked, her arms circling his neck.

"Then this'll be our last kiss," he said, and her lips pressed hard against his, her tongue caressing frantically, then she finally drew back.

"It won't be. It can't be, not for you, my knight of the handsome countenance, not for us," she said and clasped her hands to his face.

"Then you'd best start riding," he said, and she stepped back, her face suddenly all seriousness. She turned and headed for the stables, and he waited, let her saddle up, and watched her ride from the ranch. He had the shorter journey, and when he had the Ovaro saddled, he sent the horse south toward the border. He made a wide circle to avoid Vargas's compound, and it was late afternoon when he crossed the border to the north, rode across land that was mostly flat, made of sand and basalt, and he crested the succession of low dunes that stretched out before him. He thought about Vargas. The man would be on the move with his army by now. They'd not be able to make fast time with the Texas cotton-beds carrying the heavy carronades, and he counted on that.

Vargas would leave Celia at the compound, he

was certain, to wait for his victory summons, and Fargo's lips drew back as Isabella swam into his thoughts. Her own moment of truth was drawing closer, and he had already decided it would be best to let her face it alone. Nothing good would come of adding embarrassment to her pain, and he felt a rush of sympathy for her sweep through him. But it was a moment that had to come to her, in one way or another.

His thoughts of Isabella broke off as the row of uniformed soldiers crested a rise in front of him, a Mexican army patrol resplendent in dark blue uniforms with gold trim—lots of gold trim, he smiled. An officer leading the column carried a sabre in an engraved metal scabbard, his cavalrymen armed with single-action rifles, probably Spanish made. He sped the Ovaro forward to meet the patrol, and the officer waved his men to a halt. *"Hablar inglese?"* Fargo asked, drawing on his rudimentary Spanish.

"Un poco," the officer answered. *"Americano, no?"*

"Sí," Fargo said.

"What are you doing in Mexico?" the officer questioned.

"I want to see your *commandante*," Fargo said. *"Pronto."*

A half smile crossed the officer's face. "Is that so?" he said. "And why would you want to see Commandante Carena?"

"I've something very important to tell him, from the government of America," Fargo said. *"Muy importante,"* he added.

The officer thought for a moment, studying the big man on the handsome Ovaro, and then he turned and spoke to his men in rapid-fire Spanish. Two of his soldiers on sturdy, good-looking black mounts detached themselves from the column, beckoned to Fargo, and he followed as they set off at a fast canter. After perhaps a half hour he saw the sand-colored clay outlines of the army compound rise up in the late afternoon sun. The green, white, and red Mexican flag flew from one of two flagstaffs, the banner of Hidalgo on the other. The *commandante* obviously believed in the inspiration, and maybe the power, of history. Inside the outer clay walls, many of the buildings were wood, Fargo noted, including the long stables and barracks. The two soldiers led him to a row of sun-baked clay structures, halting before the tallest one with a regimental flag flying from the top, where they dismounted and waited for him to follow.

He was led inside a simple building with unadorned walls where another soldier came out, spoke to his escorts, and disappeared into an inner office. He returned in a moment and motioned for Fargo to follow. Fargo drew a deep breath and hurried after the soldier. If he could pull this off, he'd not only stop Vargas and a potential Mexican–American crisis, but perhaps establish a new climate of friendly relations. Buchanan ought to give him a medal if it worked. But he knew he'd have to avoid a number of pitfalls that could derail the whole thing. If he couldn't avoid them, Vargas would win and be able to take on Grady's men when they arrived.

He stepped into a square office as the sun began to lower outside, and a tall man in a crisply pressed uniform faced him from behind a desk, black hair slicked down, an aquiline nose and a thin pencil mustache, a slightly disdainful air to him, and Fargo winced inwardly. "I am Commandante Carena," the man said stiffly. "You must have impressed Lieutenant Cordos for him to let you come here."

Fargo brought out the note from Buchanan and handed it to the *commandante*. The man read it, ran a forefinger over the Presidential seal, and regarded Fargo with a long, speculative stare. "What is it you think I can do for you, *Señor* Fargo?" he asked.

Fargo decided only bluntness could shake the man's attitude. "It's what I can do for you," he snapped. "I've come to save your ass, to put it frankly."

The *commandante's* eyes hardened. "I hope you've something to go with your sharp tongue, Fargo," Carena said.

"There's an army of trained mercenaries marching to attack your garrison," Fargo said.

Carena's frown held disbelief. "My men patrol the entire Pinacate region. They would have seen an army being trained."

Fargo drew a deep breath. "They were trained and equipped in Arizona," he said and watched Carena's face darken.

"In America? My government will consider that a hostile act," the Mexican commander said.

"President Buchanan knows that. That's why he sent me down here, and now time's running out for you. They're on their way. They'll attack come morning, I'd guess. A man named Rolando Vargas leads them."

"I've heard the name. He is a fool, a nothing," Carena said.

"This fool has five hundred men. What's your field strength?"

"Three hundred and sixty men," Carena said.

"Shit," Fargo hissed. "They also have cannon."

"Artillery field pieces?" Carena frowned.

"Damn near as good. Naval carronades on wagons. You'll be outmanned and outgunned."

The Mexican commander offered an amused little smile. "And you have, I presume, not only come with this astounding story but a solution," he said deprecatingly.

"No solution, just some help. I've sent for the American cavalry detachment at Gila Bend. They'll cross the border tomorrow to support your troops," Fargo said.

"You have asked an American cavalry detachment to enter Mexican territory without permission? This is a story too bizarre to be believed. It seems to me that your government has allowed an army to train in your country to invade Mexico, and now you are making a last-minute effort to escape blame. If there is such an army, we will take care of it, and then we will investigate the rest of this strange story."

"There *is* an army, and you won't be taking care of it by sitting and waiting," Fargo said.

"And what is your military advice, Fargo?" Carena asked disdainfully.

"Go out and attack, surprise them. That's the one thing you can have going for you," Fargo said.

"We will surprise them by being ready right here. We have a fine defensive position here," the *commandante* said.

"Not fine enough," Fargo said.

Carena smiled again, almost chidingly. "Let us see if morning brings an army," he said. "I should dislike putting an emissary of the President of the United States under arrest. I shall accept your word as a gentleman that you will not try to leave."

"You have it. I wouldn't miss tomorrow's show for anything," Fargo said, returning his own disdain.

"My aide will show you to your quarters," Carena called after him, and Fargo followed the soldier to a small building alongside the commander's quarters. Night had descended, and the aide lighted a kerosene lamp that illuminated a neat room with a narrow bed, a dresser, and a huge clay bowl of water.

"What about my horse?" he asked the soldier who frowned back. *"Caballo,"* Fargo said.

"Sí," the man said and pointed out a window. Fargo saw the Ovaro being led into one of the long stables. He nodded as the man left, and Fargo sat down on the narrow bed. It had not gone well. The *commandante* was plainly too conceited for his own good. He was also too full of national touchiness. But it hadn't been a total loss, Fargo pondered. Carena was not a complete fool. He'd have his men ready come morning. Vargas wouldn't have the advantage of complete surprise. Be grateful for small favors, Fargo told himself as he rose and opened the door of the room and let his eyes sweep the base. Most of the barracks were already darkened, and he was about to turn back into the room when a woman appeared with a tray of food for him, a light bean soup and some spiced strips of beef.

She waited until he finished. *"Decir el commandante gracias,"* he said and she half bowed and hurried away. Fargo closed the door, undressed, and pulled sleep to himself. He wanted to be up with the first flush of dawn, and he did exactly that. Washed and dressed as the sun began to rise higher, he hurried outside and saw Carena directing his troops. He had some fifty of them on a stone walkway below the top of the walls, all hunkered down out of sight. Most of his troops were standing beside their horses, ready to charge out at the first command.

Fargo walked to the stable where no one stopped him from saddling the Ovaro, and when he emerged, he found the commander waiting on his elegant black mount. "You see, I am not entirely discounting your story about an army, my friend," Carena said. "If there is such a collection, we'll surprise them by a direct volley, and then my men will charge out at them."

"No good," Fargo said and drew an angry stare from Carena. "I told you, they'll outgun you. They'll pour fire into your men as they charge out. You ought to have all your cavalry back of the base. They're sitting ducks in here."

"They'll still be outgunned outside, according to you," the *commandante* said.

"At least they'll be able to maneuver, maybe outflank Vargas's men," Fargo countered. "He has carronades. They have to be silenced."

"Carronades mounted on wagons. How heavy a shell can they fire? Three pounders, perhaps four pounders. Our walls can easily withstand that," Carena said. "No, they won't help him. He'll have to close with his soldiers, and we'll strike from safety."

Fargo argued no further. Carena was convinced of his own strategy, and Fargo stayed as the commander rode to shout up at four of the men on the walkway. They peered through little apertures in the clay wall, Fargo saw. "Call out the minute you see something," he ordered, and the men nodded back. Fargo dismounted to stand beside the Ovaro as the hot sun rose into the morning sky. Carena stayed atop his mount with stiff military fortitude, and the morning slowly slid away. He turned a lifted-eyebrow gaze at Fargo as the sun reached the noon sky. "I must say you do not seem concerned," Carena said. "In fact, you look almost relieved."

"Yes. The later they arrive the more chances that Major Grady will get here in time," Fargo said.

Carena gave him a slightly chiding smile. "You realize that if this is all some wild story made up for God knows what reason that I will have to place you under arrest."

"I suggest you think about staying alive," Fargo growled and turned away. Less than an hour had passed when one of the lookouts called out, excitement in his voice, then another joined him. Fargo watched Carena climb up to the walkway and peer through the openings, and he moved the Ovaro forward toward the entranceway to the base. Moving toward him, still a distance away, a long line of horsemen stretched out, followed by another line and still another. Fargo waited, watched, his eyes narrowed, and he saw the Texas cotton-bed wagons come into sight, canvas tops still down, and more horsemen behind them. He felt movement at his side and saw the *commandante* there.

"My apologies, *Señor* Fargo. There is indeed an army, a sizable one," Carena said.

"Get your cavalry out of here. You've still time," Fargo said.

"No, we are protected in here. The walls are thick enough, I told you. We are protected in here. He will have to bring his men in close. We'll charge out, strike, and race back inside before he can do much. The closer he has to come with his men, the more we can bring down from in here," Carena said and backed his mount away. Fargo watched him go to his officers and explain what he planned to do. Fargo's eyes then turned to the approaching horsemen. Vargas had them outfitted with green tunics with gold buttons, which made them look a

138

little like an army though each rider wore his own trousers. He stayed watching as they drew closer, and he glimpsed Vargas on a skewbald mount, directing the wagons to draw closer to the compound in two groups. When they rolled to a halt, they were almost flanking the front wall.

Carena ordered two squads of his cavalry to form at the front gateway, but still within the compound. "Fire," he shouted to the troops on the walkway. They rose at once and released a series of volleys that took Vargas's men by surprise, a good number dropping from their horses as they tried to get away. "Charge!" Carena addressed the two cavalry squads. "Hit hard and return." Fargo watched the Mexican soldiers race into the open, holding two almost parallel tight formations with massed firepower. They brought down another twenty of Vargas's men who were still trying to get away from the rifle fire from the wall. They turned, fired off another round, and raced back to the compound. Fargo counted only two lost and three wounded.

It had been a successful maneuver that used the gunfire from the wall, a hit-and-run strike, and the element of surprise. It wouldn't have the same results twice, he muttered inwardly, but saw Carena prepare to repeat the maneuver. Again, the fusillade erupted from the top of the wall, and the two squads charged from the compound. But Vargas had drawn back and regrouped, and the volleys from the wall missed more than they hit. Carena's two squads were met by smaller units of Vargas's horsemen who came at them from both sides. But the Mexican marksmanship was superior, and they brought down a good number of their attackers as they wheeled in formation. Yet when they raced back through the compound entranceway, Fargo saw that only half returned. Carena sent another two squads out, and they engaged more of Vargas's cavalry in their sweeping, concentrated firepower circle. Once again, they did real damage, but not more than half returned.

Fargo spoke up as he saw Carena prepare to send another two squads out. "You can't keep doing this. You're losing too any men," Fargo said.

"They are losing more than we are each time," Carena said.

"Yes, but not enough more. He can afford to lose more. He outnumbers you by two hundred some men," Fargo said.

"Our attacks will even that out," Carena said and ordered two new squads to attack. Fargo watched as they raced out of the entranceway at a gallop to be met by a concentration of rifle fire Vargas had brought to bear on the gate. As soldiers toppled from their mounts, the others milled around, lost more men, and finally raced back into the main interior yard. Carena's medical corpsmen were very busy, and Fargo saw the commander's lips drawn in tightly. "They have effectively counter-maneuvered," he said. "But there is a rear gate. We will come around from the rear and strike. I'll use more men this time."

"Commandante!" one of the men at the wall cried out, alarm curled in the single word.

Fargo went to the entranceway with Carena to see Vargas's men pulling the canvas tops from the wagons to reveal the carronades, three men inside each wagon to handle each gun. Vargas stood beside the first wagon, half hidden at the rear, but Fargo saw him raise his arm and bring it down in a short motion. "Our walls are too thick," Carena grunted. "Let him use up his shells." He had just finished the sentence when the carronades roared, and Fargo saw the high, arching trajectory of the canisters.

"Shit," he bit out as the canisters struck inside the compound, exploding in a deadly hail of lead shot. He heard the cries of men and horses as the interior courtyard became a hell of grapeshot impossible to avoid except by sheer luck. Another volley of exploding canisters came down, and Fargo pulled back from the front entranceway as Vargas's men poured rifle fire into it should any of Carena's men try to race out. Carena had dashed into the interior of the compound, trying to direct his traumatized men. Fargo gave him credit for foolish courage and concern for his men.

"Against the walls, against the walls," Carena shouted. "Get out of the center of the yard." Fargo moved the Ovaro into the compound as another volley of canisters came down to fill the air with flying lead shot, and he saw some of it pepper the interior walls and a half dozen of Carena's men go down.

"Into the stables. Get your men into the stables," Fargo shouted at Carena and saw the commander turn, blood streaming from the right side of his forehead where a lead ball had grazed him. His eyes wide with shock, he nodded and shouted orders to his men who, some still in the saddle, others on foot, ran along the sides of the walls to the stables. Fargo waited till they had all reached safety, and his lips drew back in distaste as he surveyed the interior of the yard. Carena had lost at least fifty men, he estimated. Vargas had never intended breaching the walls. That's why he had used only the antipersonnel canisters. Fargo cursed the bantam rooster's cleverness.

The carronades had fallen silent and so had the stream of rifle fire directed at the front entrance.

Fargo moved past the slain men and horses that littered the courtyard and reached the stables. Carena had rallied his men, and they were calmed down, some in the saddle, others beside their horses. Carena, drying the blood on his temple with a kerchief, managed to project determination through the shock still clinging to him. "I think he has used up his carronade ammunition," the *commandante* said.

"He may have another round left," Fargo said. "He couldn't have carried much more in those wagons."

"He's waiting now, but he can't wait forever. If he wants to win, he'll have to move in to attack. The positions will be reversed. We can cut him down as he moves into the compound," Carena said.

Fargo turned Carena's words in his mind. They held good tactical logic. Vargas's men would have to come into the compound to win. Yet Fargo felt the uneasiness inside him. Celia had been right about Vargas. He was a damn good field general and a wily tactician. He'd know it would cost him heavily to fight his way into the compound. He had some plan to reduce that cost, Fargo was certain. But what? Even as he asked himself one question, the other question spiraled through him. Where the hell was Isabella and Major Grady? If they didn't arrive, there wasn't much doubt about the final outcome. He dismounted and went into the yard, grimacing again at the scene of carnage as he hurried along the wall and climbed up to the walkway where he peered over the top.

Vargas's men had spread out in a half circle between the wagons, but there was no one in the wagons, Fargo saw. Sweeping the scene again, he found Vargas in the center of the half circle. He was seated on the ground as were more than half his men. Fargo frowned. They seemed to be waiting for something, confidently, almost casually, and Fargo cursed the little man. He swore silently at Carena, also, but not in the same way. Instead of moving out to meet Vargas, as he'd been told to do, where his better trained and better led cavalry could have made a running fight of it, Carena had let himself be trapped in his compound. He had counted on walls his foe had planned to ignore. He had let himself feel superior and invincible. He'd let his flaws as a man interfere with his judgment as a commander. But he was a concerned and dedicated officer, and Fargo felt sorry for him. But history was full of good men who had fallen to brilliantly ambitious little tyrants.

Fargo turned off his musings to scan the scene outside again. Hardly one of Vargas's men had moved. They were simply waiting. He swore again and dropped to the ground where Carena had sent a detail out to clean up the yard as best they could. Fargo passed them and walked into the stable where a rear door had been opened and half the men and horses had moved outside. Carena leaned against the corner of a stall, the strain showing in his eyes. "It seems you have been right about everything, my friend," the Mexican commander said. "Except perhaps the most important thing, your American detachment."

"They should have been here by now," Fargo said grimly.

"In another few hours it will be night," Carena said. Fargo nodded and felt the sudden explosion inside himself.

"Night," he echoed, biting out the word. "Night, that's what Vargas is waiting for." Carena's eyes widened and he stared back at Fargo. "He's figuring to bring his men in on foot under cover of darkness. It'll be damn near impossible for you to pick them off. They'll dig in and be inside when Vargas mounts a full attack come dawn."

"We'll have to stop them, hand-to-hand combat. I'll have the men out there waiting in the dark," Carena vowed. It might well be his only option, Fargo realized, but it'd mean losing more men, and he couldn't afford that. Fargo turned away, grimly aware he'd nothing better to offer, and he strode back into the yard, cursing fate and whatever had stopped Isabella and the major from arriving.

He led the Ovaro toward the entranceway, then left the horse a few yards back as he dropped to one knee and peered out. Vargas hadn't changed position, he and his men still waiting. Fargo's eyes scanned the scene again, trying to find something he could use, some weakness to exploit. But he found nothing. He was about to turn away when he saw Vargas leap to his feet and spin around. The men nearest him did the same, and then Fargo heard the sound, the clear, bright notes of a bugle sounding the call to charge. He shouted as he whirled and leaped onto the Ovaro, and Carena came from the stable. "They're here," he said. "This is it, now or never."

Carena whirled and raced into the stable, shouting orders and reappeared on his black mount. Outside the compound Fargo heard Vargas's men moving to face the onrushing cavalry detachment. "You attack, full out," he said to Carena. "They'll be caught in a cross fire."

"Sí." The commander grinned. "A classic example." He raised his rifle and turned to the soldiers lined up behind him on their mounts. "Adelante!" he shouted, and Fargo put the Ovaro into a gallop beside him as they charged out of the compound. The sound of rifle fire filled the air, and Vargas's cavalry moved forward to battle Grady's troops. They went down like wheat cut by a scythe at the first volley from the Mexican troops. Some turned, quickly cut down, while others tried to flee to both sides as they realized they were trapped. Fargo could see the American cavalry now, moving in a cross pattern as they fired, taking a heavy toll as they did. Vargas's mercenaries were showing the shallowness of their training as they panicked, concerned more with saving their skins than rallying to fight.

They broke off to run in small groups, and Fargo saw Carena's men pursuing some and Grady's cavalry chasing down others. He spun the Ovaro as three of Vargas's men came charging at him, each holding an old Hawkens plains rifle. Fargo let them draw closer, raise their rifles, and try to draw a bead from their wildly charging mounts. He slid from the saddle and drew the Colt at the same time, hit the ground rolling as the Ovaro went forward, and heard two of the shots whistle harmlessly through the air. Back on his feet, he fired as the three riders yanked their horses to a halt to turn and fire again. Two of them went down as one, almost colliding as they fell. The third had managed to bring his rifle up as he stopped, and Fargo flung himself sideways, rolled, and the shot slammed into the empty sandy ground. The Colt barked as he came to a halt, and the man toppled forward, clutching his belly, fell against the saddle horn, and hung there for a moment before dropping from the horse.

Fargo ran to where the Ovaro had halted and leaped into the saddle, his eyes sweeping the battle scene. Vargas's army was on the run, decimated by the cross fire, pursued south by Carena's troops and north by Grady's cavalry. Fargo swung his eyes across the distant sandy rise and saw the lone horseman racing away. He had no need to wonder who it was. He put the pinto into a gallop and gave chase up the first rise, then the second, the pinto closing distance fast, and now he could plainly see the small, paunchy figure, his green uniform coat flapping in the wind. Fargo urged the Ovaro faster, and the horse responded at once as Vargas cleared a rise covered with creosote bush. Fargo came almost abreast of the fleeing figure before calling out. "Give it up, Vargas," he shouted and with some surprise saw the man pull up on his horse.

Fargo reined to a halt facing him. Vargas's puffy face was surprisingly calm as he walked his horse forward. Fargo drew his Colt as he saw the Remington five-shot double action revolver in the man's hand.

"It's over. It was a goddamn fool idea in the first place," Fargo said.

"It would have worked except for you," Vargas said. "Mexico would have been mine."

"Maybe," Fargo said. "Then maybe not." Vargas halted his horse, and Fargo saw the barrel of the Remington aimed at him. The Colt was already aimed at Vargas's chest. "You can't win. The Colt's hammer action is faster than that old Remington. So's the bullet speed. I can turn you over to the Mexicans or to the United States Army. I'll give you that choice," Fargo offered.

"The Mexicans will put me before a firing squad. The Americans will put me in chains for twenty years. Hardly much of a choice," Vargas said.

"More of a choice than you were going to give me," Fargo said, his voice hardening.

"Men of vision have no time to offer choices," Vargas said with sudden pompous arrogance. Fargo's finger began to tighten on the trigger of the

Colt as he saw Vargas raise the barrel of the Remington. But the little man continued to raise the gun until it was under his chin. The shot drowned out Fargo's cry of protest. Rolando Vargas flew backward from his horse, and suddenly the gray-green creosote bushes were flecked with red in a wide arc.

"Cowards haven't got the guts to take choices," Fargo murmured as he turned the Ovaro and began the ride back. The battle had ended when he reached the compound, and he saw those left alive of Vargas's mercenaries being shackled to each other. Carena and Major Grady stood talking to each other, and he saw the slender figure with the jet black hair standing by. She was in his arms the minute he swung from the saddle. "Took you long enough to get here," he muttered.

"My fault," Major Grady cut in, a stocky man with a broad, reddish-complexioned face and clear blue eyes. "I had half my men out on patrol when she arrived. I had to wait for them to get back or come with fewer than a hundred men, and I don't think any of us would have wanted that."

"You're right there," Fargo said.

"Vargas got away," Carena put in.

"No, he didn't," Fargo said. "He was a damn fool to the end." Both the major and Commandante Carena nodded without pressing further.

"I thank you, *Señor* Fargo, and you, Major," Carena said. "*Presidente* Juarez thanks you. But I think perhaps it would be best if this became something that never happened."

"I'm sure President Buchanan would agree with that," Fargo said. "It'll be an unwritten paragraph in history."

"Exactly," Carena said. He and the major exchanged salutes, and he offered a firm handshake to Fargo before he led his men away with their prisoners.

"My mother," Isabella said. "Now we can get her."

"Can you take Miss Downing to the compound, Major?" Fargo asked.

"I'd be happy to," Grady said.

Fargo met Isabella's questioning eyes. "I think it's best you do this alone," he told her as he groped for words. "There may be things you'll talk about that you won't want me knowing," he added, and she shrugged. "I'll wait for you at the ranch," he said. She brightened at the prospect and went off with the major. Fargo watched her go, a slender figure moving with youthful grace. He'd be at the ranch to help her cope with the truth she'd have to face. Celia Downing would have her own defeat to wrestle with. She'd not be gentle with Isabella.

He climbed onto the Ovaro and slowly rode north, back to the ranch.

10

The night was deep and the ranch dark when he reached it, and after stabling the Ovaro, he went into the guest room and welcomed sleep. He rose early though he didn't really expect Isabella would appear before noon, and he wondered if Celia would be with her. He got his answer much earlier than he'd expected as he'd just finished a cup of coffee in the kitchen when he saw the lone figure riding hard toward the ranch. He waited in the kitchen as Isabella, black hair flying in the wind, a rifle in her hand, drew to a halt and all but leaped from the saddle. She entered the kitchen, and he saw the dark fury in her face.

"Bastard," she flung at him. *"Plebeyo!"* He was already diving behind the table when the shot slammed into the wall behind him. He rolled through the doorway at his back as another shot sent a spray of wood from the door frame. "You rotten, stinking bastard," he heard Isabella shout as he kept rolling into the living room and dived behind the heavy sofa. "Betrayer. Judas," Isabella shouted as she followed.

"You can't blame me for what she did," Fargo said. "I tried to tell you she wasn't a prisoner."

"Goddamn you," Isabella said and fired again, the shot high and smashing into the wall. She paused to reload, pulling cartridges from a pocket in her skirt, and he saw an open window just behind him. He half rose and flung himself headlong through it. "Come back here," he heard Isabella shout. He hit the ground, spied a water trough beside some small sheds, and hurled himself behind it as Isabella came out the side door of the house.

"Dammit, you blaming me for being right?" Fargo called to her as she advanced with the rifle.

"Not for being right, for being a lying, double-tongued *fullero*," Isabella shouted. "You slept with her, you bastard. You slept with my mother. You slept with Celia."

Fargo swore silently as first surprise, then anger swept over him. He hadn't expected Celia to be that much of a bitch. "She tell you that?" he asked Isabella.

"She said it enough."

"What's that mean?"

"She was very upset at the way things turned out, especially you. She said you would have been so right for her. You were so good in bed, she said." Isabella's voice broke, and in fury she fired another shot. Fargo ducked, stayed for a second more behind the water trough, and then raced in a crouch to the nearest shed. "I hate you, Fargo. I hate you," Isabella shouted as she came after him. He ducked around the corner of the shed and paused. She was consumed with fury and hurt. He'd expected her to be hurt, but not this way, and she was fighting back for that world she had created for herself. He heard her coming closer and darted around the corner of a second shed as she followed behind the first, half sobbing and half cursing.

Moving on silent steps, he came around the rear of the shed and across the back of the first. She was ahead of him, now, moving slowly. "Come out, damn you," she sobbed. He moved quickly, three silent steps, and his arms were around her, wrestling the rifle from her and throwing it aside. He twisted away as she tried to claw at his face, and he pinned her arms behind her and pushed her against the shed. "How could you?" she sobbed in fury. "How could you?"

"Listen to me, goddammit," he said, holding her. "I'm not your Don Quixote. I'm nobody's knight in shining armor. I never was. You made me that." Her eyes looked at him with wounded anger, and he let her arms go and held her by the shoulders. "There are no knights anymore, not in this world. There are just men, imperfect men with faults and flaws. The best of us do more good than bad, the worst of us more bad than good, but we all do some of both. That's all there is. It's not the way you want it to be. I'm not. I never was."

She stared back, and suddenly the doe brown eyes were filled with tears and she was sobbing pitifully into his chest. "You shouldn't have, you shouldn't have," she said.

He didn't try to justify anything. That would have been dishonest, and she didn't deserve dishonesty. Maybe she didn't deserve reality, either, but he had nothing else to offer. "It happened," he said simply.

"You promised you'd be faithful," she sobbed.

"You promised yourself that," he said gently, and she blinked at him through her tears. He held her and only stepped back when she drew away, her face still tear-stained, but the fury gone from it.

"I want some time alone," she murmured. "Maybe we can talk later."

"I'll stay till tonight," he said and watched her walk into the house, her slender figure stooped as though all the weight of the world was upon her. He picked up the rifle after she left and put it in the house, then spent the rest of the day washing some clothes and drying them. The burning Arizona sun would dry them in a matter of hours. When the sun finally slid across the horizon with the riot of red-orange, yellow, and deep purple he had come to expect of the southwestern sunsets, he prepared to leave as one of the kitchen workers came to him.

"Eat something first, *señor*," she said, and Fargo agreed and sat down to a meal of venison stew and tepary beans. He was almost finished when Isabella appeared; she wore a long, loose dress. Dry-eyed, she sat across from him, and the woman brought her a shot glass of tequila.

"You don't have to leave," she said.

"Thanks, but it's best I go," he said.

"Where?"

"Toward Gila Bend and then northeast into Colorado," he said. "Is Celia coming back here?"

"Probably," Isabella said.

"Are you staying?"

She shrugged. "I don't know." Her doe brown eyes held an infinite sadness as she searched his face.

"It was so wonderful," she said, and he knew what she meant.

"It was, and no one can take that away," he said.

"Everything is different now," she said.

"Not just because of that," he told her.

"It was the most important part," she said. "I've thought of all that's happened, all the things you said this morning. They were all important, but that was the most important." She finished the tequila and rose, stepped to him, and leaned over. Her lips were soft and gentle on his, and then with sudden ferocity her tongue darted out wildly, caressing, and her hands dug into his shoulders. But she pulled away, her breath coming in deep gasps.

She spun and strode from the room, somewhere inside the long, loose dress.

"Take care, Isabella," he said softly after her, but she didn't turn. He rose, finally, gathered his things, and rode from the ranch in the darkness under an almost full, burnt orange Arizona moon. He didn't hurry as he rode along the north edge of the Growler Mountains and found a spot against a stand of ajo oak to bed down. He had undressed in the warm night and lay near-naked on his bedroll, listening to the sounds of elf owls that nested in holes in the saguaro. He was almost asleep when his wild-creature hearing picked up another sound, hoofbeats, a horse moving slowly.

He sat up, his hand on the Colt in its holster alongside the bedroll and watched the horse come into sight. The dark shape moved toward him, and then the moonlight fell on the rider and the shock of black hair. He sat up, and Isabella reined to a halt and swung from the saddle. He saw she wore a riding skirt and a blue shirt that rested against the long curves of her breasts. "You are not the only one who can follow a trail," she said.

"Seems not," he agreed.

"I have a cousin in Colorado. I'll stay a while with her. I thought you could take me there," she said.

"Why not?" He nodded.

"That wasn't all of it," she murmured, her eyes peering at him from lowered brows.

"Go on."

"There was too much for forgetting and not enough for remembering," she said, sinking down on her knees beside him.

"You think hard about this?" he questioned.

"Very hard, about all of it, everything that happened, and I knew one thing above all else. I cannot let you go, not yet. You mean too much to me."

"Me, Skye Fargo, no shining knight, no Don Quixote."

"That's right, you, just you," she said, unbuttoning her shirt. "No more wanting for knights, just nights for wanting."

"Now, that's growing up," he said as he pulled her to him and her breasts came onto his chest. It would be a trip made of good deeds, very enjoyable good deeds. After all, wasn't that what a knight was supposed to do?

1860, Colorado Territory—
where the high Rockies
can be as snow white
and beautiful as a woman,
and just as cold
and treacherous . . . .

The bitter wind of late autumn carried the smell of wood smoke. Skye Fargo awoke and raised his head, sniffing the cold afternoon air warily, his nostrils flaring. Yes, there it was again—the odor of a fire, and something cooking. Unmistakable and not far away. He cursed himself for having fallen asleep.

Fargo turned over, remaining in a recline and careful not to rock the birchbark canoe. Between slitted eyes he slowly scanned the ragged shoreline. While he'd been napping in the sun, his canoe had drifted the length of the long mountain lake, and now he was close to the edge of the lake. The blue spruce crowded their trunks right down to the water, while off to one side a stand of quaking aspen rained their golden leaves in the slight breeze. He expected to see a canoe drawn onshore, or a campsite. But there was nothing.

Whoever was camped nearby had hidden the site well. Too well, Fargo thought uncomfortably. And, whoever it was had built his fire so that it burned almost smokeless, at least to the eye. But as his canoe drifted nearer shore, the acrid odor of fire was so strong, Fargo knew he was practically right on top of whoever was there on shore.

Who would be up in the high country this late in the season anyway? He was miles away from the gold mining stakes far to the west in the broad valley. But maybe some prospectors had wandered into the area. He discounted this idea immediately. Miners were usually slovenly, making camps you could spot from the next territory. Utes, he thought. Some straggling Utes who hadn't yet gone over the high pass to their winter camp in the Never Winter Valley. Fargo suddenly felt uncomfortable and cursed himself for falling asleep on the lake. He started to put his hand to his Colt, but then realized it would be a mistake.

Whoever was there knew the ways of wilderness and was, at this very moment, looking out at Fargo's drifting canoe from the cover of the dark recesses among the spreading branches of the spruce. One shot and he was done, Fargo thought. And whoever it was could pick him off like a floating duck. On the other hand, somebody camped so invisibly among the spruce could just want solitude and no trouble. Fargo realized he'd have to take that chance. There was no other choice.

Fargo sat up and stretched his arms above his head and yawned loudly as though just waking up. He pulled his fishing line out of the water and made a great show of disappointment at the empty hook. He lifted one of the six speckled golden cutthroat trout that lay in the bottom of the canoe and held it up to look at it. Then he lifted his paddle. In a moment the canoe was gliding swiftly across the clear water away from the trees, leaving a subtle wake behind him like the point of an arrow.

As he paddled, he felt the twitching between his shoulder blades and his muscles were tense, ready to spring into the water at the least sound from behind him. But nothing moved, and the gunshot never came. When he'd gone halfway across the width of the lake, Fargo began to relax.

Since he was in full sight of whoever had been camped there, Fargo didn't head to his campsite tucked among the rocks at one end of the long lake. Instead, he beached the canoe on some rocks on the opposite shore. He strung the fish on some line and turned away, plunging into the dark spruce forest.

He'd been riding through the high country of Colorado for a week, making his slow way down toward Denver City to pick up some more work. He wasn't in any particular hurry, not with a thousand dollars in his pocket from his last trailblazing job. Instead, he'd taken a detour over Blackblood Pass and lingered in the big valley, feasting on trout and enjoying the clear chill air and late golden aspen of autumn. He'd planned to stay by the lake one day more before riding out, back over the treacherous pass, the only route in and out of this part of Colorado Territory. He'd already stayed longer than he'd planned, and the first snow of winter would come any day now.

Fargo climbed halfway up a low-limbed pine and hung the string of fish up high, well away from the sharp claws and teeth of any wandering black bears. Around him the golden-headed ground squirrels scrambled up the branches and searched among the fallen logs as he sprinted farther up the slope. They hardly noticed him as he turned and hiked through the dense trees along the ridge. They were intent on their work, fat with the nuts they'd eaten, their fur thicker than usual. It would be a bad winter in the high country, Fargo thought. All the signs were there.

Rather than heading back to his campsite, Fargo had decided to pay a visit to the unknown visitor. He'd angle around the lake, keeping in the dense trees for cover, then creep in and get a look at him. If he was going to remain camped by the lake for the night, he'd better get a look at who was staying nearby.

In a half hour Fargo slipped silently through the white papery trunks of the aspen on the hill above the hidden camp, toward a stand of blue spruce. He reached the darkness of their trunks and headed down the slope toward the shore. The sun was setting and the water had cooled so that the breeze had reversed, the wind coming off the lake now, so he was downwind of the camp. He dodged among the trees until finally he stopped behind a large trunk and peered into the somber darkness ahead.

He caught the flicker of fire and, as he watched, movement. An old man in fringed buckskins stood up and rotated a long stick with gobbets of sizzling meat over the flames. An old spotted mare stood to one side, and Fargo was glad for a shift in wind. If he'd still been downwind, the horse might have smelled him and given the alarm. Fargo studied the dim figure before him—long lanks of gray hair and a gray beard. A pile of pelts lay to one side of the fire.

Satisfied, Fargo silently withdrew, retracing his steps up the slope. The man was a trapper, an old-timer, traveling alone. Harmless enough. And, although curious to talk to him, Fargo knew the etiquette of the trail—never to burst in on a man's camp unless invited or unless you gave fair warning. Not unless you wanted to taste his lead.

But the old trapper had secreted his campsite so carefully it was clear he wasn't interested in visitors. Fargo would respect that, now that his mind was at ease about his identity. Fargo had gone only a short ways, and the sun had just set over the mountain when he heard whoops and gunfire behind him in the direction of the trapper's camp. Fargo halted and listened as the sounds reflected clearly off the water. Several men, with guns. It was an attack.

Fargo wheeled about and sprinted back toward the campsite, drawing his Colt. He plunged down the slope through the dense spruce until he saw the yellow fire flickering ahead. Fargo halted and dashed from one tree to another, coming closer and closer until he crouched behind a rotting log within twenty feet. He rested the Colt on the log and sighted down the barrel.

Two men held the old trapper by the arms, but it was impossible in the gloom to see their faces. The third, a huge blond one, poked at the pile of pelts.

"Nice haul," the blond one said. "Beaver, elk, bear, even."

"Just take it if you want," the old man said. "And there's some greenbacks and gold in that buckskin bag over there." The blond man looked over toward where the old man was pointing and grinned. "Take it. Take it all, but leave me in peace. I ain't done nothing to you. Hell, I don't even know who you are."

"How much you think we can get for these?" the blond said, still bending over the pile of skins.

"Shut up, Jake," another answered. "Just get on with it."

Jake spun about and fumbled at his belt, grabbed something, and raised his arm high. Fargo peered in the dim firelight to see what the man was holding. It was a tomahawk.

"Now, where do you suppose those bloodthirsty Utes would bury this?" Jake said in a nasty voice, circling the trapper. The old man struggled in the grasp of the other two. "In the forehead between the eyes? Or maybe in the back of the skull?"

Fargo didn't wait for Jake's next words. He pulled the trigger, and Jake pitched sideways with a yelp, grabbing his thigh. The other two men threw the trapper to the ground and took a step backward, bringing up their guns. Two bullets thudded into the log, just below where he'd crouched, but Fargo had already rolled along the ground several yards, keeping behind the log. He came up again, gun blazing, and caught one of the men dead center, before ducking behind a tree trunk. Fargo melted into the shadows beneath the trees and sprinted in a short arc around the campsite to come behind them. Their confused shouts and shooting covered the occasional snapping of branches.

He eased himself around a thick tree trunk and looked out. Jake lay swearing by the fire, holding his bleeding leg and his gun in one hand, trained on the trapper who sprawled on the ground. The other man was firing wildly in the direction from which Fargo had shot.

"Go after him, you idiot!" Jake shouted, his voice an agonized shriek.

The man started forward just as Fargo stepped closer. His boot came down on a dry twig that snapped like a rifle shot. At the sound the man turned about and fired wildly into the trees where Fargo stood. Three bullets whizzed by him, and Fargo crouched, advancing and dodging. His Colt spit fire again and again, and the man screamed in agony. Just then there was a flurry of movement in the firelight as the old trapper sprang up and vaulted toward Jake and the other man ducked away. Fargo dashed forward into the small clearing. The trapper and Jake struggled by the fire, the other man nowhere to be seen.

Fargo cursed and kicked out, catching Jake's big gun hand as he brought it around behind the old trapper. Jake's pistol flew up, and the trapper pinned Jake's arms, sitting astride him. Jake's leg was bleeding bad, blood darkening his jeans and the ground under him.

"I'll go after the other one," Fargo barked at the trapper.

Fargo slipped into the trees, listening intently. He had only gone a few yards when he heard the whinny of a horse from high up the slope. He realized the three men had come on horseback along the high ridge above, and the third man had got away.

With a curse Fargo returned to the campsite. Who the hell were these men anyway, he wondered. He'd get the answer out of Jake.

The old trapper was still holding Jake down, but as Fargo came up, he saw that the blond man didn't have long to live. The old man, seeing Fargo, got up and stood looking down at Jake.

"Oh, God, I'm going to die," the blond man muttered, his face pasty and drawn. The blood was pumping hard out of his leg, and Fargo unwound the kerchief from his neck to make a tourniquet, then realized Jake had also been shot in the chest, probably in the tussle with the old man.

"Who sent you here?" Fargo shot at him.

Jake's clouded eyes focused slowly on Fargo.

"Goddamn redskins," he said, anger in his voice. "Living off the white folks. We'll show 'em." His tone of voice changed as he started to go out of his head. "Oh, Mama. I'm going to die, Mama."

"Who sent you here?" Fargo snapped again.

But Jake was beyond comprehension. He muttered incoherently for another few moments, then his head fell to one side and he gazed, blank-eyed into the fire.

"The other one got away," Fargo said. "Their horses were up the hill."

"Thank you, stranger," the old trapper said. "My name's McCain. I'm obliged to you. I spotted you out on the lake."

Fargo nodded and stood over Jake, looking down. The old trapper spoke his thoughts.

"I hoped he might live awhile," McCain said.

"You recognize any of them?"

McCain shook his head.

"But I'd sure as hell recognize that mustachioed one again, that one that got away," he said, spitting into the fire.

Fargo nodded. He hadn't had a good look at the man's face, but he wished he had. And he didn't like the three men's having found the old trapper's campsite, since it had been so well hidden. The three had been dangerous. And he hoped there weren't more of them around.

"There's something real bad about all this," McCain said. Then he was silent as if he'd said too much.

"They weren't after your pelts," Fargo said. "Or your money. They just wanted to kill you and make it look like the Utes got to you."

McCain nodded silently, his eyes narrowed.

"Let's move your camp away from here," Fargo said. "In case that mustache comes back with some pals. I'm camped over by the rocks to the north. I could use some company."

McCain nodded and set to packing up the camp. In a matter of moments he had smothered the fire and loaded the pelts onto the dappled mare's back. Meanwhile, Fargo knelt and riffled through Jake's pockets. He found a knife, a few gold dollars, and a penny postcard, which Fargo held to the light.

Even in the quivering firelight the woman's face was beautiful—her dark brows arched high and her full lips parted slightly in a teasing smile. But what drew his attention was the rest of her. She was dressed in a scanty merry widow that showed off her tiny waistline. The lacy garment was cut low and clung to her deep cleavage, barely hiding her nipples. She stood in front of a painted palm tree, with one foot on a carved chair and a shawl over her upraised thigh, which was artfully draped to hide her charms. Her legs, slender and shapely, weren't bad either. Whoever she was, she wasn't shy about showing what she had.

Fargo turned the card over and found an inscription on the back: "To Jake, from Lily. Hurry back."

Fargo pocketed the card and returned the rest of the contents of Jake's pockets. He felt around the man's thick belt. Three more small tomahawks were tucked into his waistband. Fargo removed one and held it up to the light. The jagged-mountain symbol and the red lightning across the haft marked it as Ute.

Fargo dropped it and stood. McCain waited by his mare, ready to go.

"I haven't even asked your name."

"Fargo. Skye Fargo."

The old trapper nodded.

"I might have guessed that," he said with a smile. "I've heard all about you. You've done a helluva lot for a young fella."

"Let's get a move on," Fargo said. There'd be time to trade stories later, he thought. For the moment his only thought was to return to his own campsite as quickly as possible. The light had nearly gone from the sky, and he suddenly felt worried about his own gear and his pinto hidden at the far end of the lake. They started off quietly in the gathering dark.

Fargo retrieved the string of cutthroat trout from the tree where he'd left them. He angled down toward the shore intending to check on the canoe. When he got there, he found it filled with water, a huge hole in the center, where somebody had put a boot through the birchbark bottom. A Ute tomahawk was buried in the wooden frame. Fargo saw confused tracks on the shoreline, but he didn't pause to examine them closely. Every moment counted now.

They hurried toward Fargo's camp and with every step, he knew he was arriving too late. As he neared the tumble of rocks, they left McCain's mare in the trees and approached on foot, scrambling silently over the boulders as the stars came out overhead. With silent gestures Fargo signaled McCain to stay behind as he ventured forward around the rock cropping and into the concealed vale where he'd camped for the past three days.

It was as Fargo had feared. The gear in his saddlebag had been scattered and picked through. Nothing much was gone. A sharp glance told him that his trusty Sharps rifle still hung almost out of sight among the golden-leaved branches of a nearby aspen. His bedroll had been sliced to pieces, and another of the Ute tomahawks was buried in it.

The black-and-white pinto was gone. The hoof-prints, cut deep in the grassy bank, showed the horse had struggled when the strange men tried to lead it away.

Swiftly, Fargo gathered up his belongings and packed them into the saddlebag. He retrieved his Sharps from the branch and rejoined McCain a moment later.

"They got you, too?"

"And they're not interested in stealing," Fargo said. "Just killing and stirring up trouble against the Utes. But who? And why?"

He puzzled for a few minutes over whether Jake and the two men might have hit his camp first and then gone on to wreck the canoe and swarm down on McCain. But he'd been out in the canoe until heading over to spy on the old trapper. And, if Jake and his two had hit Fargo's camp while he'd been napping on the lake, the Ovaro's neighing would have carried across the water and he would have awakened. His faithful pinto never went anywhere with strangers without putting up a helluva fuss. That meant there had to have been two parties of men. The second party hit his camp at the same moment as Jake hit the old trapper. The noise of the gunfire had hidden the distant sound of the horse's call.

The thin mountain air had turned cold. Fargo donned a wool shirt and topped it with his buckskin jacket.

"I guess I'll track them in the dark," he said.

"Count me in," McCain said.

Following tracks in the rocky soil in the pitch black and a cold mountain wind, only his burning anger and the thought of the black-and-white pinto in somebody else's hands kept Fargo going, hour after hour.

At times he crawled on his knees on the pine-needle carpet, peering into the darkness until his eyes made use of the dim starlight above. Only once or twice did he resort to lighting a match, since the light blinded him and it took long minutes for his eyes to readjust to the darkness once the match snuffed out. McCain followed in silence, leading the mare.

There had been four of them on horseback. Four against one. Fargo wondered if he'd have managed to survive if they had found him in camp. And also, how the hell they'd found him anyway, hidden among the rocks. Whoever they were, they were damned good.

They had climbed the slope up above where the canoe had been and passed several miles through forested country, emerging to circle the shore of another, smaller lake. Then the tracks wound down a mountainside and along a rock ridge, where the prints would have been impossible to trace even in broad daylight. Fargo was losing hope. They stopped finally at the bottom of the slope of scree on a broad meadow. Fargo walked back and forth in the starlight, looking in vain for the dark smudge of the horse's tracks.

"Let's start again in the morning," McCain said. Fargo knew the old trapper was right. Even if they did find the trail, the four horsemen and his Ovaro were riding fast. They were miles and miles away by now.

"There's a Ute summer camp not far from here,"

McCain said. "Standing Elk's tribe. They'll have gone over the pass to the Never Winter Valley already, but we can take shelter there."

McCain led the way, and in fifteen minutes they were approaching a narrow canyon, choked with low dark piñons. Fargo could smell the coming winter in the stiff wind in his face. The first snow would be coming soon, he knew. And the snow fell hard up here in the big valley. If he stayed too long here, searching for the Ovaro, he risked being snowed in when the only pass, Blackblood Pass, was buried. He shook the thought away. McCain pushed his way between the small low trees, moving silently and warily. McCain stopped as the canyon walls narrowed and Fargo came up alongside him.

McCain inhaled and Fargo did, too. There it was again, the smell of wood smoke. Maybe two days old.

"What the hell are they still doing here?" McCain whispered. "They should have moved on out a few weeks ago."

Fargo inhaled again.

"But no cooking odor," he said under his breath. "Old smoke smell. And the smell of . . . "

He left the words unspoken, but he knew McCain had identified the smell, too. The old trapper turned and tethered the mare to a pine. Then they both drew their pistols and edged forward, moving like a pair of shadows in the darkness.

Burned flesh. That's what that smell was that hung so horribly in the cold night air. The smell of burned human flesh and hair was unmistakable.

They paused at the edge of the piñons and looked

out across the grassy bottomed canyon. A half moon rising over the mountains to the east spilled light across the meadow, and Fargo saw the dark, ribbed skeletons of tipis and small wickiups. The two men stood looking for a long time in silence, their eyes slowly gathering in the details, the lumps of dead bodies on the ground, the charred circle of grass that extended nearly to the pine trees where they stood. At the far side of the meadow Fargo saw movement and he tensed, then realized there were a few horses there. Whoever had attacked the Indian village hadn't even bothered to drive off all the stock.

Nothing else moved. After a long time Fargo started forward and McCain followed at a distance to cover him.

The Utes had been gruesomely murdered, hacked, and burned. Many had been shot in the face. Fargo picked his way across the ashen wreckage, noticing that each of the bodies had been skewered with a Ute lance or a tomahawk.

"Same bunch," McCain said grimly.

"Trying to make it look like Ute killing Ute," Fargo said. "Could it be true?"

"Utes are as sharp as a knife blade," McCain said. "Just as dangerous. But straight as a honed edge. No Ute would turn against another tribe. And not Sitting Elk's. He is . . . was . . . a powerful chief."

Suddenly, Fargo's keen ears picked up a slight rustle. He gripped his Colt and shot a look at McCain. The old trapper nodded. He'd heard it, too, and it came from the direction of a burned-out wickiup, which was nothing more than a charred pile of sticks leaning on each other. But with enough room inside the wreckage to hide somebody—somebody still alive.

"Come on out," Fargo said as McCain moved off to the side to cover him. He spoke the words again in the Ute dialect, which resembled the language the Shoshoni and Paiutes used.

A sharp sound came from the wickiup, and then all was still again. Fargo repeated his words, adding that he was a friend and came to help. Finally, he walked a few steps nearer. Suddenly, a figure leapt out at him. Fargo saw the flash of a blade in the dim light, and he grabbed at the arm, twisting it easily.

"Let go. Drop it." He grabbed the figure around the waist and felt the softness of her breasts and hips. "You're safe."

The knife dropped to the ground, and the woman collapsed beside it. Fargo picked up the blade and handed it to McCain, who walked up next to him and stood looking down as the woman sobbed.

"Where is Sitting Elk?" McCain asked in Ute dialect.

At the words the woman looked up. The starlight fell across a delicately featured face and round black eyes framed by long tangled dark hair.

"Beaver Man!" she said. She wiped her face with the back of her hand and struggled to her feet.

"Waiting Cloud!" McCain said. "You are lucky to be alive. Who did this?" The old trapper turned to Fargo and explained, "This is Chief Sitting Elk's daughter."

At his words she stiffened, and the fear crossed her face again. She swallowed and tilted her head upward as if to regain herself.

"Most of my people have gone already to the Never Winter Valley. But I waited here for my father. He rode away three days ago," she said. "To talk white talk with men from the powerful white chief. He was not here when the . . . when the fire death came. White men with Indian weapons brought the death."

"So, Sitting Elk's alive," McCain said.

"There's time to talk later," Fargo said. Just because the chief was not at camp when the attack came didn't mean he was still alive. And the sharp smell of death hung like a cold curtain in the chill night air. "Right now, I think we should get out of here. Go find a safe place to camp."

"No place is safe," Waiting Cloud said mournfully. "No place is safe."

"You will be safe with us," Fargo said. "Wait here and I will find horses."

He set off across the meadow and soon returned with a string of four strong horses—one each for him and the woman and two extra for McCain's pelts and supplies. In the wreckage of one tipi he spotted horse gear—Ute leather bridles and several of the high-seated, elaborate Spanish-style saddles the Utes used. Fargo chose the smallest of them.

When he reached the two of them, Waiting Cloud was kneeling in the ashes, moaning and swaying in the moonlight. Fargo and McCain withdrew to the edge of the pine trees, redistributed the saddle bags and pelts onto the Indian horses, and waited. After a time Waiting Cloud arose and joined them without a word.

Fargo handed the reins of the string to her.

"These horses belong to you," he said.

"Four horses?" Waiting Cloud said, looking him over. "But I am the daughter of a chief. Have you anything else?"

Her words weren't making sense, Fargo thought. But he decided to humor her. Beside him McCain shuffled and looked down at the ground.

"The same men who killed your people, stole my horse," Fargo explained to her. "But we have some food and guns. Come with us. If you let me ride one of your horses, we will get you to safety."

"Four horses, some food, and a gun." She looked at him a long moment, flicking her hair with one hand over her shoulder. She grasped the mane of the nearest horse and swung herself up. Her buckskin dressed hiked up, and her long, muscular legs were dark against the horse's pale coat. "I accept your offer," she added. "I will call you Dark-of-Night."

Waiting Cloud turned the horse's head toward the piñons and kicked its ribs, and they were swallowed by the dark pine branches.

"What the hell?" Fargo said.

McCain stifled a chuckle.

"Is she in her right mind?" he asked the old trapper.

"Sure," McCain said. "You came up and gave her four horses. And she accepted your offer. You just bought yourself a wife, Fargo."

"*A what?*"

"Yep. Your wife, Waiting Cloud. Daughter of the big chief. You and Sitting Elk will get along real well. You treat Waiting Cloud right, and I'm sure you and the chief will get on just fine." McCain clapped him on the shoulder and was having a hard time not bursting out into laughter.

"This isn't funny, McCain."

"Sure it is," the old trapper said as he mounted a horse and rode off after her, leading the two pack horses. "Sure it is, Mr. Dark-of-Night," he called over his shoulder.

"Goddamn it," Fargo muttered. All of a sudden he was saddled with an Indian wife, daughter of the big chief no less. And somebody had run off his Ovaro. And he was now mixed up in something big and ugly—a bunch of men rampaging through the big valley, tracking and killing indiscriminately, whites or Utes. And snow on the way, a bad, deep winter that would seal off the valley.

It had been a helluva day.